What readers think

MW00977429

The Delaware Press Association has awarded *First Time* second place for the best collection of short stories by a single author in their 2017 Communications Contest. Evaluation comments from the literary judge follow:

"The stories in this collection engage immediately. Each story comments of a memory of that very first time - who doesn't want to remember college and loves? A tender look at mid-life, and end of life experiences. The stories written in first person capture the reader's emotions."

There is something for everyone here

First Time contains a variety of stories beginning with four dopey college students driving to Florida for spring break and ending with my favorite, a touching story of a widower re-tracing the last vacation he took with his beloved wife, Anne. It's a good collection and an excellent way to get to know the author, Frank Hopkins. *R. E. Reece on August 15, 2016*

...book of short stories entwining each one together...

I enjoyed reading how you can relate to past experiences in some way to your own life...I certainly could especially...Santa Claus Stories and My Trip Alone...these stood out for me. *Judith L. Kirlan July 29, 2016*

First Time is nostalgia at its best.

The variety of stories touch on some part of a

reader's own life, from a spring break trip to an exotic love. Frank E. Hopkins does a fine job of weaving the stories that, at first seem to stand on their own, but then all come together. Each story taps into the emotions of events throughout life in a way the reader can relate. All-together, *First Time* makes a great beach read with each story taking just a little of your time. I recommend it. *Jack Coppley June 13, 2016*

First Time is a witty, eclectic, entertaining collection of memorable times
Author Frank Hopkins' creation "First Time" is a witty, eclectic, entertaining collection of memorable times in the lives of ten individuals. First impressions are always the lasting impressions and "First Time" will make a pleasant dent in your enjoyment psyche. *Amazon Customer May 17, 2016*

…being reminded of similar firsts from my youth
…fond memories as a student or the traditional Spring Break trip to Florida. The bitter sweet memories of my first car and a trip alone. But by far was a memory I didn't have but could live through his writing, the trip to Sorrento. Beautifully written, through his words, I enjoyed the walk up from the beach, the breeze from the sea and the aromas coming from the multiple restaurants he visited. I could feel the charm of the city in his writing. *William Kennedy April 13, 2016*

…will make a pleasant dent in your enjoyment psyche.
Author Frank Hopkins' creation "First Time" is a witty, eclectic, entertaining collection of memorable times in the lives of ten individuals. First impressions are always the lasting impressions and "First Time"

will make a pleasant dent in your enjoyment psyche. *An Amazon Customer on May 17, 2016*

Hopkins Always Keeps You Hungry For More

Reading "First Time" by Frank Hopkins was my own first time with the author's short stories. I'd devoured his Hoffman-O'Hare detective novels and was anticipating more of the same, only in a shorter format. What a disservice I did him. I had no idea his range was so far-reaching, well beyond the parameters of a mystery novel. Here were characters of all ages beginning with naive college freshmen, burning red after eight hours on Daytona Beach, still enjoying their first spring break. At the ending was a man, two years after his beloved wife's death, on a sentimental journey to their time-share in the West Virginia Mountains.... Each tale reflects Hopkins' fascination with the human psyche. You can almost hear him ask "What makes this guy or gal tick?" And as he works it out, the reader also enjoys a veritable travelogue of colorful locations. *Mary D on Jan 3, 2020.*

You Won't Put This Book Down Until Completed.

Totally entertaining book. The ten short stories appeal to everyone. Interesting and fascinating book written from the male point of view. Especially touching is "My Trip Alone" because it is a story that most people have to go through. "My First Psych Course" was funny and so true with college courses. Everyone remembers their first experiences, and this book is a collection of memories for all. I actually could not put the book down, anxious to read the next adventure. Hopefully, Frank E. Hopkins will repeat this achievement with more short stories. *Sally*

Scarangella on April 10, 2018.

First Time A collection of enjoyable short stories by Frank E. Hopkins

First Time is a collection of short stories written by Frank E. Hopkins. He delves into the lives of his characters beginning with college students taking a cross-country excursion to visit the south. I enjoyed the way the author portrays the lives of different characters dealing with romance, marriage, divorce and death. The reader is able to identify with several of his characters. I chose "My Trip Alone" as my favorite. It is a story of a middle aged man who courageously forces himself to retrace the last trip he and his wife took together prior to her death. This is an uplifting story of renewal as the story evolves, ending with renewed hope for a new beginning in his life. I thoroughly enjoyed reading this story and recommend it. *Ruthziemniak on Jan 29, 2020.*

FIRST TIME

SHORT STORIES

FRANK E HOPKINS

Other Books by Frank E Hopkins

Fiction:

>*The Counterfeit Drug Murders*
>*The Billion Dollar Embezzlement Murders*
>*Abandoned Homes: Vietnam Revenge Murders (*
>*The Opportunity*
>*Unplanned Choices*

Non-fiction:

>*Locational Analysis: An Interregional Econometric Model of Agriculture, Mining, Manufacturing and Services,* with Curtis Harris.

No part of this book may be reproduced in any form or by any electronic or mechanical means including information storage and retrieval systems, without permission in writing from the author. The only exception is by a reviewer, who may quote short excerpts in a review.

This book is a work of fiction. Names, characters, places, and incidents are the product of the author's imagination or are used fictitiously. Any resemblance to actual events, locales, or persons, living or dead, is coincidental.

Text Copyright © 2021 Frank E Hopkins
All rights reserved.

ISBN-

Ocean View Publishing
Ocean View, Delaware

DEDICATION

To my Daughters: Karen and Linda

Table of Contents

ACKNOWLEDGMENTS

I would like to thank the Salisbury Critique Group of the Eastern Shore Writers Association and the Rehoboth Critique Group of the Rehoboth Beach Writers Guild for reading and advising me on how to improve several of the short stories. Maribeth Fischer helped improve my writing skills in her classes by teaching the art and importance of dialogue, setting, and point of view in fiction. Jackson Coppley, Walt Curran, and Bill Kennedy read beta versions of the book, and provided invaluable insights and recommendations for correcting errors and improving the readability of *First Time*. Numerous individuals provided significant help by reading and commenting on individual stories in the book, including Mary Lou Butler, Kathy Haven, Wendy Lippincott, Carl Pergler and Jerry Sweeney. I want to thank Sally Scarangella, who performed the final copy editing, identifying errors and suggesting improvements in the manuscript. Michael Nicholson of DW Design, Inc. produced the cover which captures the main theme of *First Time*.

Passages South

Passage One

When I, Bill O'Malley, attended Hofstra University on the brink of adulthood in 1964, I drove from Flushing, Queens, New York City, to Daytona Beach, Florida during spring break. Four of my friends, John, Larry, Ralph, and Tim, who went to St. Johns University in Queens, accompanied me. We went in search of warm weather, experiencing southern culture, learning how to surf, and our main goal of meeting co-eds. The trip started on a cold March Friday morning with a cooler packed with beer and lunch. The danger of driving a car with New York license plates in the South and being caught and hung by the KKK concerned us. We had a real fear since in the 1960s southern headlines reported the killing of northern Freedom Riders, church bombings, and

Civil Rights marches stopped by southern sheriffs using attack dogs.

The Delmarva Peninsula where I have now retired to live had racial tensions which began in Cambridge, Maryland in the early 1960s, culminating in riots in 1967. They destroyed much of the downtown, the scars of which still remain. Anyone born after 1970 might not appreciate our fear and the violence of the Civil Rights struggle.

We planned our trip to Florida well in that age before GPS systems. We obtained route information, maps, and motel reservations from the American Automobile Association. The AAA travel plans helped us avoid the southern speed traps and minimized contact with the southern police. In the 1960s the country had a much lower standard of living compared to 2012. However, even college students with summer jobs could afford the trip of 1,050 miles since gas cost 29 cents a gallon, and we shared moderate motel expenses. We hoped to complete the long ride in twenty-four hours with two seated in the front and three in the back in a large 1958 blue four-door Bel Air Chevy. We stuffed our luggage in the trunk and strapped two surfboards to the roof. We took turns sleeping and driving with a strict rule: each driver would quit drinking four hours before driving. Few interstates existed in those days, and we drove on two-lane rural roads and an occasional four-lane divided highway. These roads lacked lights and were bordered by irrigation ditches. Since we never had complete darkness in the New York City area, several of us experienced our first dark nights with bright stars. The Milky Way astounded us.

After driving four hundred miles, we stopped for dinner on a rural Virginia highway at a restaurant with a prominent Stuckey's sign on its roof. After enjoying a southern dinner of fried chicken, mashed potatoes, and string beans, we started to leave when Ralph discovered Stuckey's flagship product pecan nut rolls. He purchased several. After taking a bite he exclaimed, "These are great! Have some."

Ralph twisted off several pieces and handed them to us. We smiled after biting into the candy.

"We'll have to stop there again. Did you notice there were no Blacks, either customers or help in the restaurant?" Tim said,

"This is the segregated South." Larry replied.

We missed our twenty-four-hour goal by several hours because of a communication problem and a driving mistake.

A gas stop in North Carolina surprised us. In those days gas stations were called service stations and attendants pumped gas. When the attendant, dressed in an oil-stained uniform, came to the driver's side of the car, Ralph said, "Fillerup wid regula," in his 1960s Brooklyn accent.

The attendant gave us a quizzical look and replied in unintelligible words.

None of us could understand him, nor he us. We felt we were in a foreign country, and I'm sure he considered us from a different world. Each of us tried enunciating our words but after our first attempts, we reverted to using our fingers to communicate. Ralph pointed at the regular gas pump. He raised his hand high which the attendant understood and filled the gas tank. I won't describe the signals we used to convey our need to visit the restroom.

We observed the country as we drove further south. The land turned to red clay. Housing became differentiated between the respectable wood frame painted houses and the small tattered tar paper and unpainted wooden shacks. The large homes, set far from the road, surrounded by late-model cars, and acres of farmland, had a few whites entering or leaving them. Fifteen feet by thirty feet unpainted homes were located less than fifty feet from the rural two-lane road. These shacks had no cars, only black children from toddlers to teenagers, and an occasional adult, all dressed in frayed, faded clothing. The shacks shocked us. We remained silent. We had black friends in New York, who lived in respectable middle-class housing. These homes were our first real view of the impact of racism and poverty, outside TV, and our visits to the segregated slums of Harlem and South Jamaica, Queens. New York had housing far superior to the ramshackle dilapidated homes of the black south. We talked about Civil Rights, an uncommonly mature discussion for us, until we fell asleep.

The driving mistake occurred around three a.m. in the moonlit South Carolina night. I woke up with my head hitting the car ceiling and the car bouncing. When I looked out the window I noticed we had landed in a ditch. The driver Larry spoke when asked by his four scared companions what had happened, "I saw headlights coming straight at us so I swerved the car right and went into the ditch."

"Let's get out and examine the car," Ralph replied first.

The two foot deep ditch contained a few inches of water. John and Larry, our surfers from California, examined the status of the surf boards on the roof. John said, "Thank God, they're still okay. If they fell off and broke, our vacation would be ruined."

Never having surfed, I didn't share their relief.

"Let's try to push the car out. We don't want to wait for the police, it might take hours, and we don't know what they'll do," I suggested, expressing everyone's fear.

Larry steered the car, and we four strong nineteen and twenty-year old men pushed it forward.

We soon realized this approach got us deeper into the ditch, and the spinning wheels of the rear-wheel drive vehicle sprayed us with mud.

"This isn't working, let's push it backward," Tim said.

Larry took his foot off the gas. We went to the front of the car and pushed it up the hill as Larry lightly pressed the gas pedal. The strong reverse gear moved the car onto the shoulder of the road

After finishing, we took a deep breath and tried but couldn't wipe all the mud off our clothes.

"Larry, we're on a divided highway. It's impossible a car with oncoming lights could have forced you off the road, unless they drove in the wrong direction. Are you sure you weren't asleep?" Tim said.

"I don't know, but I saw the headlights and thought I saved our lives."

"It doesn't matter. If a car did or didn't drive in our lane, you were asleep and gave us an early morning workout. Even though you still have an hour of driving left, I recommend Bill drive, it's his turn, if he's not tired," Ralph said.

"I'm okay. I'll drive, but we should give up beer until we arrive since we don't want to get stopped with beer on our breath and mud on our clothes," I said.

We agreed. I drove through Georgia, giving

up the wheel when we passed Jacksonville, Florida.

Within six hours of leaving New York, we had discovered another difference between Long Island and the South. Our trip started with the windows closed and the heater on high. As we drove south, the car became hotter so we reduced the heat to stay comfortable. However, we had to turn it up as the night chill grew. We turned it off in southern Georgia at sunrise. Since our 1958 Chevy lacked air conditioning, we opened the windows by eight a.m. as the temperature rose to escape from the hot stale air reeking of spilt beer and the aroma of five sweaty, muddy, young men. The heat became our first happy vindication of why we left a cold New York.

After arriving at the Daytona motel, we explained our adventure to the clerk who looked at our mud-stained clothes in disdain. He verified our reservation and reluctantly let us sign-in.

We stayed in an old rundown former apartment building located two blocks from the beach and a quarter of a mile north of the Daytona Ocean Pier. The apartment had two bedrooms, a living room, and a kitchen. Having our priorities straight, we brought the cooler in before our luggage and immediately chugged a beer to celebrate our safe arrival and avoidance of the KKK. Each bedroom had two single beds and the living room had a pull-out sofa. We flipped coins to assign the beds and the order of taking a much needed shower. I won the sofa bed and the first shower. After showering, unpacking, and drinking our second beer, we skipped lunch and crashed.

At four p.m. after waking up, we visited the beach which differed from Jones Beach, New York. "At home there's either a sand bar a hundred yards out where the waves break, or no sand bar, and the waves crash on the beach. Here the beach is flat and the breaking waves run for a long while before they dissipate," I told the others.

"That's why we came here. Unlike Jones Beach, the waves here are perfect for surfing." Larry answered.

Seeing beautiful girls clad in bikinis, instead of the women wearing heavy winter coats in cold New York again vindicated our decision to go south. We talked to a few, and I asked a slim blond, clad in a string bathing suit, "We're looking for something to do tonight. Do you have any ideas?"

"Go to the Pier. There's a band and dancing there. The band starts at nine. I'm Jean. My friends and I'll be there," she said pointing to the Pier.

Jean introduced her friends, and I identified myself as did the others. The girls came from Indiana, students at Purdue. We impressed them by talking about our New York origins and our enrollment at St. Johns and Hofstra. Well, St. Johns anyway, they'd never heard of Hofstra. I promised Jean that I'd tell her about Hofstra at the Pier.

We left the Purdue women at five-thirty. We were famished since we had skipped lunch and walked to an all-you-can-eat restaurant recommended by the motel clerk. Upon entering, we noticed we were forty years younger than the other all-white customers, our first experience at meeting the retired segregated population of Florida. Looking at the $6.50 buffet, we knew we would not leave hungry. The first twenty-foot table, included salad, rolls, vegetables, mashed potatoes, fried chicken, fried fish, and pork chops. A chef stood to the left at a separate table, carving a round roast. A third table to the left of the round roast displayed desserts.

Our famished stomachs forced us to the first table where we loaded up on salad on one plate and other food on the second. We filled our plates several inches high while the senior generation ate healthier portions. After finishing our first serving, we went for seconds including a separate plate for desserts. None of the senior generation had seconds.

On Saturday night, we slept well after overeating and dancing with the Purdue women and arrived at the beach in the early morning. Before leaving our rooms, we slathered ourselves with suntan lotion and spent most of the day looking at girls, talking to a few. We didn't see the Purdue women during the day, but looked forward to meeting them at the Pier after dinner. The sun attacked our skin for eight hours except for our short break for lunch at a boardwalk eatery. Late in the afternoon, we realized everyone had cherry red skin.

On Sunday evening, we returned to the restaurant repeating our first evening's performance. We walked back to the motel slowly in severe pain and stayed at the motel room that evening and decided against taking showers, knowing drying ourselves would be too painful.

I called Jean's motel, and when she answered, I said, "Hi, it's Bill. I had a great time last night. You're quite a dancer."

"Thanks, you're good too."

"Unfortunately, we stayed on the beach too long today. We're hurting with severe sunburn and can't meet you tonight."

"You sure you didn't meet another group of girls and are dumping us?"

"No, we're intrigued by you and your friends. We don't have farm girls in New York City."

"Well, I planned to tell you tonight. We've going to an Ohio State party on Monday evening. One of my friends dates an Ohio State student. If you want to join us, meet us on the boardwalk at the front of the Pier tomorrow night at eight. There won't be any food at the party, just beer kegs so have dinner before we meet."

"Thanks. We'll be there."

"Good, please don't go to the beach tomorrow, you don't want to get worse. Go easy on the beer, since it'll dry out your skin and make the pain worse."

"Okay, you're the pre-med. See you tomorrow night."

I relayed the invitation and medical advice to the guys who looked forward to the party. They said they'd follow her advice to stay out of the sun, but since she was only a pre-med major, and didn't have a medical degree, they ignored her advice on drinking.

After waking up from a painful restless sleep, we again decided not to shower, stayed in the room most of the day reading and playing cards. My bathing suit felt tighter on Monday morning. My friends experienced the same phenomena. We wondered if the humid Florida air shrunk our clothes.

Around noon, severe itching added to the pain of the sunburn. I left my room and asked the desk clerk, "How can I stop the itching?"

"Use calamine lotion. You can buy it at the drug store across the street," he replied.

The itching stopped, but I smelt like the calamine bottle. I told the others to use calamine lotion to treat their itching and by early afternoon everyone emitted a body odor similar to mine.

On Monday evening, when we entered the

restaurant, the manager walked over to us and said, "You must leave. We won't serve you."

Tim our pre-law student asked, "Why."

"I don't have to tell you."

"This is a public restaurant, licensed by the city. You have to serve us." Tim replied.

"You're not in New York. Read the sign by the door. It says, 'We reserve the right to refuse service to anyone for any reason.' Those words are approved by the city," the manager said.

"We'd still like to know why" Tim replied, stymied.

"Have you looked in the mirror today? You look like bums. It's the third day I've seen you. You'll get pudgy if you keep gorging yourself. We charge you $6.50, but you eat over twice as much food as we budget. We can make a profit with our genteel clients, who have healthy appetites, but not with you college student gluttons. You're ruining your vacation. Even northern girls don't like fat boys."

"I guess it's not the humid Florida air," I said as we left the restaurant.

We heeded the restaurateur's advice and ate healthier the rest of the trip.

With the enthusiasm and confidence of youth we dressed for the party in spite of the sunburn's itching without showering. We planned to meet the Purdue women and consummate our new relationships. We arrived at the boardwalk first. The girls arrived a few minutes later and stared at us.

Jean, still twenty feet away, asked, "Is that a New York hair style?"

"No, we couldn't wash our hair because of the sunburn," I replied.

"You guys have BO and smell like a medicine cabinet," Jean said as she got closer.

"The sunburn itched so we rubbed ourselves with calamine lotion," I explained.

"You guys stink worse than my father's pig sty, and your hair looks worse than our dogs after they've rolled in the mud," another girl commented.

"I don't think we can take you to the party, you'd gross everyone out, and ruin our reputation, if the word got out we're your friends," Jean said. The other girls nodded their heads in agreement.

They turned around and walked to the party while we stood amazed at their unreasonableness.

"At least they didn't complain about our beer breath, like my girlfriend does," Tim said.

"It's undetectable because of the lotion," Ralph commented.

"They're not for us. Midwesterners are too Goody-Two-Shoes for New Yorkers. They don't understand our suffering. The evening would have been a bust," Tim replied.

We knew they had helped us avoid a disastrous

evening. For whatever reason, we met no other women that evening as we strolled on the boardwalk and patronized a few bars. We never saw the Purdue women again.

The next day we felt better, rubbed on more calamine lotion, but still postponed showering until the itching stopped so as not to aggravate it. We experienced cabin fever from staying in the motel during the day, so we went to the beach after lunch. Still in fear of the sun we wore our jeans and long sleeve shirts and doused our faces with thick white suntan lotion.

As we walked the two blocks to the beach, we noticed women watching us. I said, moving my head looking around, "Forget the Purdue women look at the women staring at us."

"You're right. Let's see how we do today. We'll even get more babes after we start surfing," Larry commented.

We spread our blankets between several groups of bikini-clad women and flirted with them. Most of the women acted shy and reserved in their conversation, excusing themselves to go swimming. We couldn't follow them since we didn't want to expose our peeling sunburned skin to painful salt water. After two hours of these interchanges and fear of damaging our handsome faces with more sun, we went back to the motel.

It's surprising we couldn't connect with anyone," Larry said as we walked back.

"Maybe it's our clothes. They weren't Florida beach attire," I suggested.

"I doubt it. Several people wore protective clothing," Ralph replied.

"Yeah, but they're in their sixties, like those in the restaurant," Tim said.

"Maybe they're just tired from partying and from being hit on," I said.

We returned to the motel. As I walked into the bathroom, I viewed myself in a full-length mirror. The image wasn't me but that of a Bowery bum. This shocked me and made me think no wonder we're alone. The itching faded away as I showered and washed the mixture of dried calamine lotion and the sweat off my skin, and shampooed my hair. I dressed in clean shorts and a t-shirt and told my friends to do the same. I felt rejuvenated as the others soon did.

After dinner on Tuesday, we went dancing at the Pier and met several women. At the motel, we drank a few more beers laughing at our mistaken view of our attractiveness and sexual prowess, despite how we looked, dressed, or offended others by our body odor. We embraced our new humility, vowed to shower at least twice a day, and restart the vacation over on Wednesday morning.

"Since we're healthy now, we'll begin surfing lessons at ten tomorrow. I recommend we leave the beach at noon and stay off till three so we don't get sunburned again," Larry said.

The next morning, we walked to the beach carrying both surf boards.

"Aren't those waves much higher than yesterday?" Tim said.

"Just a little but the higher the better," Larry replied.

I didn't agree.

After we had settled on the beach, Larry said, "John and I'll show you how it's done."

They both picked up the surf boards with smiles on their faces and waded into the surf. At least fifty yards out in waist high water, they jumped on the boards, lay face down, and used both hands to paddle out beyond the breakers.

"That's a lot of work, just to surf," I said.

"Both seem to love it, so it must be worthwhile, and they guarantee it'll attract girls," Tim replied.

"It might not be work to them. Let's watch and learn," Ralph said.

The gracefulness of their moves impressed us as they surfed toward us, and we noticed at least a hundred women, including some we'd met the previous night, staring at them. Each of us thought I'd like to learn to surf. I'd be irresistible.

John and Larry laid both surfboards on the sand and instructed us on how to stand on the boards. Next, they took us out to the water and showed us how to get on the boards and paddle through the waves. We were proud of our performance, thinking this must be the easiest way to attract women.

Then, Larry and John attempted to teach us how to stand up on the boards in the water. Our confidence and dreams of unlimited women vanished. As I fell off for the fourth time, Larry tried to use an associative method of teaching.

"Bill, think of standing on the board as just skiing on water. When a wave changes the position of the board, adjust your legs from the knees to stay balanced. The same way you do when skiing."

"We're from Long Island, not California. We don't have mountains. None of us have ever skied."

"Really? New England's so close."

"We play basketball and go to the beach."

"Too bad, I'll teach you next winter. It's almost noon. Let's leave before we get sun poisoning."

We felt relieved as we walked off the beach. As we passed beach blankets adorned with bikini-clad women, we noticed they did not smile, but smirked, except when they lovingly gazed at Larry and John, who returned their looks with come-on smiles.

After lunch, we stayed in our rooms, returning to the beach at 3:00 p.m. to continue our practice. By 5:00 p.m. we could stand on the boards and Larry said, "That's enough for today. I don't want to exhaust you. Tomorrow we'll surf the waves."

At dinner, Larry and John praised our performance, saying it had taken them a week to learn what we had learned in a few hours. We thanked them for their encouragement which we thought lies and promised to do better the next day. Each day we improved and by the end of the week both Ralph and Tim became proficient while I remained a beginner.

Larry and John didn't lie, surfing attracts women. After dinner on our first surfing day, freshly showered with combed hair, we visited the Pier. It astonished the three of us when women who had seen us attempting to surf besieged both Larry and John, who introduced us to their new friends, and promised to include them in the surfing lessons for the rest of our vacation.

We had a great time driving home to New York, still on the lookout for the KKK, discussing our experiences and new knowledge of women, surfing, and our plans to learn to ski next winter.

Passage Two

I have often thought of our trip and of returning to Daytona to relive my youth, but marriage, children, divorce, and career postponed my return. Forty-eight years after the first passage south, retirement in the Delaware gave me the time to retrace my original trip.

My goals for the second passage differed from the first. Many of my southern Delaware golfing friends, wintering in Florida, would send nasty-gram emails whenever we had cold weather in Sussex County, Delaware informing us they played golf in their shorts, while we dressed in overcoats. Rather than complain about the emails, I became curious whether I should visit my friends in Florida and contemplate spending my winters playing golf. I drove to Florida in December to examine the East Coast around Palm Beach and the West Coast near Naples where my friends spent their winters.

I had no interest in running after women since I'm struggling to remember my past sexual experiences. Because I'm gluten intolerant I couldn't drink beer. I avoided spending eight hours a day on the beach getting a tan, since I have spent years at the dermatologist's being treated for sun-damage. However, I wanted to discover how the South had changed since my first trip.

It took ten minutes to plan the drive from my Ocean View home to Palm Beach using MapQuest, not AAA. I stopped at Savannah, Georgia, on the drive south, and Fayetteville, North Carolina on the return trip. Whereas I had spent the first non-stop passage driving in a non-air- conditioned car on two and four-lane roads, I made the second passage enjoying an air-conditioned car with seat warmers primarily on Interstate highways.

Speeds on the Interstate are now higher, 60 to 75 miles per hour, compared to an average of 45 on the first trip so I missed many of the local population's cultural traits on the second trip. During my drive I left the Interstates for lunch, gas, and site-seeing. I tried to compare what I remembered from years ago with my new observations. Stuckey's still served lunch and sold pecan rolls, although I declined to buy any candy, since my doctor had told me I had a pre-diabetic condition. On the earlier trip I had eaten at least ten.

When I walked into the restaurant, I noticed a major difference: black customers ate their lunch served by white waiters, and black waitresses served white customers. While I knew desegregation had been legally implemented, it reassured me to see integration as my earlier personal memories had been of a segregated South. It pleased me that my country's racial problems, while not resolved, were well on the way to recovery from the situation fifty years ago. An individual who died before 1970 returning today would find an unimaginable level of racial tolerance, compared to their earlier experiences.

I stopped for gas many times on the trip and had

numerous conversations with Southerners and never had a problem understanding them nor they me.

The second visit to southern Florida made me appreciate the Delmarva Peninsula. All my New York college friends, family, and their relatives must have moved to West Palm Beach, which I found more densely populated than Brooklyn in the 1960s and more congested than 2012 Washington, DC beltway rush hour traffic.

I traveled for three hours on Interstate 75 from West Palm Beach to Naples, crossing the picturesque Everglades and the Big Cyprus National Preserve. The population of the Naples area on the Gulf Coast while less dense than West Palm Beach lacks the inland bays of Delaware and the rivers of Eastern Shore Maryland and Virginia, where I can kayak and fish from a skiff without fear of being eaten by alligators and pythons. Thus, as I am leaving middle age, I have decided to spend my next thirty or forty years enjoying the golf courses, tennis courts, ocean, bays, rivers, and natural wonders of the Delmarva Peninsula without wintering in Florida.

My First Four Days in Sorrento

On September 2012, I had just finished a two week August sail in the Bay of Naples with forty of my fifty- and sixty-year-old friends from our Annapolis Sailing Group. When I arrived in Italy, the sight of the steep volcanic mountains around Naples and on its bay islands made me sorry I hadn't visited southern Italy earlier before my retirement when I had the stamina to hike for hours.

After the sail, three of us had planned to stay in Sorrento for several days as a convenient location for visiting the ruins of Pompeii and Herculaneum.

My sailing friends told me I would love Sorrento which they thought the most scenic town in the Naples region. I wondered how its beauty could exceed that of the islands or mainland ports we visited: Procida, Ischia, Capri, Amalfi, Gaeta, and Ventotene. They had seaports with a backdrop of rugged mountains only found on the eastern coast of the U.S. at Bar Harbor, Maine. The port villages contained Roman, Medieval, and modern buildings and narrow streets.

Aboard the high-speed ferry approaching Sorrento, the sight of the town on a thousand-foot cliff above the small port, so different from the other sea level villages I had visited, overwhelmed me. I took several pictures of the cliffs and the port which I intended to email to my children from my room at the Hotel Regina.

After departing the ferry, I looked at my map to find the hotel. I stared at the cliff face wondering how to scale the rocks. The American tour guide warned me not to take a taxi since they charged 50 euros or $70. As I despaired of an easy solution, I saw a sign in English and a few other languages, *Elevator*. I followed the arrows on the sign towing a suitcase on wheels while carrying a camera and computer bag on my shoulder in the ninety plus degree heat. After I paid the fee of one euro, the elevator took me to the top of the rocks near the Church of St. Francis where I saw a wedding in progress. A great start to their new life together and my visit to Sorrento.

The map displayed the Via Marina Grande, the hotel's street, a short two-block walk. After studying a printed Internet picture of the white four-story hotel, I walked through narrow streets, just wide enough for the passage of one car, bordered by centuries-old stores and apartment buildings. Turning right at the corner of the first block, I walked several hundred feet and discovered the turquoise water of the Bay of Naples stretched in front of me. The next street to the left displayed a sign identifying the Hotel Regina. The real three-dimensional view of the hotel and the bay with the wind blowing through the trees and the smell of the sea enthralled me, far exceeding my hopes when I had reserved a room on the Internet.

After registering, I emailed my two children a summary of the morning's events and included pictures of the cliffs, the hotel, and the Bay of Naples. Eric, my son, wrote back asking, "Are you going rock climbing on the cliffs like we used to do in West Virginia and the Rockies?"

I answered "No", citing my bad knee as the only problem holding me back.

That afternoon I walked around the narrow streets and Piazza or squares, ate Italian food, drank local wine, and rested from the rigors of the two week sailing trip. Faith and Dennis, two of my sailing friends, and I stayed in separate hotels. We agreed to converge at the Fauno Bar on Corso Italia at the Piazza Tasso, the main square in Sorrento, each night to discuss our day's adventures. The bar is one of over two hundred restaurants in Sorrento.

We sat at the tables in the open area in the

front of the restaurant covered by a green awning. Both Italians and tourists strolled on the Piazza Tasso. The enclosed area at the back of the restaurant never frequented by the customers contained a large bar, twenty tables, and the kitchen. The Fauno Bar differed from the Italian restaurants we had patronized, catering to English and American tourists, not Italians. While they served Italian food, the portions were twice as large as the local helpings, paralleling the difference in waist size between the English-speaking tourists and the citizens of Sorrento. After a solid diet of traditional Italian food since arriving in Rome three weeks ago we returned to an American diet. Faith ordered salmon while Dennis chose corned beef, and I asked for fish and chips. Faith and I drank white Italian wine while Dennis ordered Chianti.

As we ate, I told them of my adventures getting to the top of the cliffs to avoid the fifty euro taxi fare.

Faith giggled, and said, "There must be a mistake in your tour guide since I arrived at my hotel fresh and ready for the rest of the day after spending five euros on a ten minute air-conditioned taxi ride."

"Dave, I had the same five euro taxi fare," Dennis concurred, as he broke into uncontrollable laughter and knocked his wine glass over spilling the red wine on the pristine gold colored table cloth.

We tried to clean the spill with water. An Italian waiter.walking by our table, in perfect English, said, "Don't worry. The tablecloths are covered with Scotch Guard so the wine won't stain."

While we drank decaffeinated espresso, we made plans for the rest of our Sorrento visit. The schedule included a local rail trip to Herculaneum the next day; an independent tour of Sorrento on the third day; and a visit to Pompeii on the fourth day; then leaving Sorrento on the morning of our fifth day.

After dinner, I strolled west to the Via delli' Accademia, a narrow street, bordered with compact centuries-old Italian stores. They sold everything: clothes, china, jewelry, leather goods, wine, meat, fish, gelato, restaurant food, and chocolate. I entered a gelato shop, drawn by bright signs and the candy displayed in the window. As I slowed and approached the gelato case, a curvaceous but thin, in the Italian style, middle-aged woman with dark hair streaked with gray followed me. She gripped my arm as she walked by and said in excellent English, "You're cold."

The tenderness of her touch warmed me. I glanced at her at her flat stomach, curvy breasts and hips.

She moved behind the gelato counter and asked, "What can I get you?"

"A cup." Pointing at a small one, I asked,

"How many flavors?"

Smiling she responded, "I can give you three small scoops."

Shaking my head I touched a larger cup, costing 4.50 euros.

"That's better. What flavors?" she said.

Pointing at several containers under the glass cover, "What are they?" I asked. After she answered, I chose chocolate, pistachio, and coffee. She scooped the three flavors and added a partial scoop of lemon, saying, "I'm treating you well in hope you return."

She walked to the front of the counter and took my hand. "Come outside."

I had no power to resist her suggestion. We walked several feet to the right of the entrance where she pointed at a small circular table. "Sit here and enjoy."

"Thanks for the gelato and the table."

"You're still cold. Shorts and a t-shirt are fine during the day, but nights are cool in Sorrento. Wear long pants and a regular shirt tomorrow night."

She turned and reentered the store, and I enjoyed the best gelato ever, warmed by the memory of her touch.

The hotel fee included breakfast on their fourth floor roof. I took a table on the outside guarded by a black metal railing and looked at the blue Bay of

Naples, a thousand feet below. Gentle waves and a few whitecaps painted the water's surface. Freighters, large cruise ships, ferries, and small fishing boats moved on the bay. The waiter brought me coffee and told me to go to the buffet to choose breakfast from the rolls, eggs, cheeses, fruits, and meats adorning the table. Before going to the food, I returned to my room to retrieve my camera to capture the soul of the bay I now loved.

While we had spent two weeks sailing the islands outside the inner bay, we hadn't sailed near the city so like any new love the inner bay stunned me by its beauty and charm.

I began by taking wide-angle pictures of the city of Naples, Mount Vesuvius to the right, and the coast to the left across the bay. Spying several of the fishing boats near the hotel, I changed to a telescopic lens and took pictures of the individual boats retrieving squid from traps, a process similar to that used on the Chesapeake Bay to catch crabs. I focused the lens to see the sun-tanned, weathered faces of the fishermen. I planned to hang several of the pictures on my study wall at home.

At nine the next evening, I returned to the gelato store, an hour before closing time, dressed in pants and a short-sleeve shirt. She greeted me, touching my arm, "You're still cold. I'm glad the lemon flavor worked to bring you back."

"I'll have the same as last night."

"Chocolate, pistachio, and coffee, plus a dab of lemon to keep you returning."

"Correct."

"Did you have a good day? Where did you visit?"

I told her about our trip to Herculaneum, the Roman ruin covered by the same volcanic eruption that buried Pompeii as she dished my gelato, handed me the cup, and took my money. She led me to the small table I sat at the night before, but instead of leaving she sat next to me, saying "It's good to talk to an American again. I'm Arabella Fabiocchi."

"Dave O'Neill. Arabella, you speak perfect English, with somewhat of a Brooklyn accent, I remember from years ago."

"As a young girl, I used to live in Brooklyn. My family emigrated from Sorrento in 1967. I went to Erasmus high school."

"In college, I went out with a beautiful teen Italian emigrant from Brooklyn. We went to see *Funny Girl,* when it first opened, but I realized she didn't have a spark for me so we never went out again."

"Well, it wasn't me. Dave, I'm sure I would have shown more affection than your date. I watched *Funny Girl* on TV with a young Irish American boy, with several of your features, who I married. The army drafted him after our wedding, and he died in

Vietnam. We had no children. My father died in a car accident a few years later, and my mother and I returned to Sorrento the following year, and I purchased the store."

I asked her questions about her life in both Brooklyn and Sorrento. She asked me about mine in America. I answered hoping to impress this Italian woman who had shared my country long ago.

After we had talked for forty-five minutes, her co-worker, approached and said a few words in Italian. Arabella repeated in English, "My niece tells me it's time to close. Wait here, don't go."

I couldn't tell whether her words were a request or a command, but I stayed, having no desire to leave even when her niece moved the table and chair into the small shop.

After Arabella closed her shop, she returned and said, "Please walk me part of the way home, it's on your way to the Hotel Regina."

I thought I knew an American woman's intentions when she asked that question, but didn't understand the silent meaning of words from an Italian woman. Enthralled, I replied, "I'd be happy to."

Taking my arm, we talked strolling down Via delli' Accademia turning right at Via Torquato Tasso reaching the Piazza della Vittoria. "The Hotel Regina is nearby, while my apartment is a few blocks down the street," she said.

I sensed we parted too soon now understanding this Italian woman had a different silent language than an American. Arabella had enticed me, and I felt I had to see her outside her shop, knowing I could talk to her forever. "Can I take you to lunch tomorrow, when you close your shop for the siesta?"

"Yes. Stop by the shop before one."

We parted kissing each other's cheeks, the formal way Italians say hello or goodbye with a more than informal hug.

Smiling, I walked to the hotel smelling the salty air and the fragrance of the lemon trees in the mountains. When I arrived, I emailed my children telling them about my trip to Herculaneum and included two photos of the ruins.

Ronnie, my daughter, emailed me back saying, "Thanks for the pictures. Take as many as you can. I want to show them to my third-grade students."

I replied that I will, but didn't tell her of my gelato adventures.

After falling asleep, I dreamed of my new Italian female friend. I slept late that morning, and impatiently waited for my first date with Arabella. As her first name promised, I wondered if she would answer my prayer to end my loneness.

I arrived at the store and had planned to ask her to pick the restaurant. Arabella greeted me warmly with a smile and a kiss on both cheeks and said, "Instead of going to the tourist restaurants I've prepared an authentic Italian meal for you."

We retraced part of last night's steps but kept going straight from where we had parted. We continued walking for two more blocks before she stopped in a residential area outside the commercial district at a three story rose pink apartment building, with no stores on the first floor, and said, "Here it is."

I followed her up the stairs, warmed by the sight of her slim attractive body. We entered her two-bedroom air-conditioned apartment on the second floor. I noticed the earthen colors of the wall, floor and furniture, including a smooth polished walnut dining room table. The colorful festive Italian china reminded me of the wares sold in the local Sorrento shops. Arabella later told me, we ate at a three-hundred year old table. She went to the refrigerator and poured an apéritif, a glass of Falanghina, a local Neapolitan white wine, and said, "Please sit on the couch. I'll be right back. I always take a shower when I return from work."

On the couch, I had a view of the Bay of Naples where on this clear day Mount Vesuvius and the Islands of Procida and Ischia could be seen. The side window faced the mountains, occasionally covered by clouds. When they cleared, the lemon trees could be seen clinging to the slopes.

Arabella returned in a loosely flowing tan dress and served lunch, commenting, "Dave, I hope you like it. Italians always have the big meal at lunch."

I assumed she meant the meal but I, loved the dress. Arabella dished the Antipasto of grilled octopus and calamari onto my plate, informing me, "The seafood came from the Bay of Naples this morning."

Contented, I ate and listened to Arabella. "I left America so long ago and only lived in Brooklyn. Do you eat fresh seafood in Delaware?"

"Yes, that's one advantage of living near the ocean, but we fry it, and it doesn't taste as good as the seafood I've eaten in Italy."

"Too bad, I liked the U.S., but I'm spoiled by our fresh food." Arabella continued talking about Italian food and culture, and I wondered why I hadn't visited Italy earlier and stayed longer.

Arabella next served the Primo dish, a non-American small helping of fettuccine alla Re Ferdinando II made with creamy ricotta and mozzarella cheeses, sweet tomatoes, basil, and prosciutto. I thought the Italians stayed thin by walking, but now I realized both reasonable portions and walking contributed to their great health.

Arabella served chicken scampi, a pounded chicken breast sautéed with white wine and lemon, for the Secondo course. We talked as we ate, taking two hours to savor each morsel of her home-cooked Italian food.

Then Arabella said, "We'll have dessert later."

I helped her clear the table. She washed the dishes, and I dried, a romantic process long forgotten in America with its ubiquitous dishwashers. After finishing the dishes, she opened the fridge door and pulled out a bottle of Limoncello, poured the golden liquor into two small chilled metal cups and said, "Dave, I'm glad I met you."

Before I could reply, she continued talking, "Drink," placing her arm on my arm and shoulder like the first night I met her. I complied and sipped my Limoncello. When we finished she said, "I have to return to work. What are your plans for tomorrow?"

"I'm touring Pompeii."

"If you'd like a guide, I can have my niece run the store."

"Yes, I'd like that."

"Good, I'll pick you up at your hotel. Driving is much faster and cleaner than taking the Naples Circumvesuviana train."

"Arabella, I didn't know you had a car."

"I only drive when I leave Sorrento."

We walked back to Arabella's shop with her hand on my arm. The warm feeling of the first night returned. Had I already lost control of my emotions. I cautioned myself to go slow. As we walked and talked, I kept thinking of my life over three thousand miles away, and how she would be perfect if she lived in Delaware.

When we reached her shop she said, "Dave, I promised you dessert. Please come by before closing."

I walked back to the hotel in a mental turmoil. I wanted to stay in Sorrento and become closer to Arabella, but the irrationality of staying and failing tormented me. When I reached my room, I followed my heart and cancelled my plane reservation to fly home in two days. I emailed my children telling them I had postponed my return since I had so much more to see. They both emailed back telling me to enjoy myself. I didn't tell them of my long lunch with Arabella.

For the third night in a row, I joined my sailing friends, Faith and Dennis, for dinner at the Fauno Bar. While we were drinking our first glass of wine after ordering, Faith asked, "What time should we meet at the train station tomorrow for the trip to Pompeii?"

"Eight-thirty," Dennis responded.

I remained silent and Faith asked, "Dave is that OK with you?"

On my walk to meet them for dinner, I had rehearsed how I'd tell them I wouldn't join them, but had not expected that question so early in the evening. "I won't be going to Pompeii with you, I have other plans."

"What! That's all you've talked about for the last week!" Faith exclaimed.

"Does it have anything to do with the Italian woman I saw you walking with this afternoon?" Dennis asked.

Blushing for the first time in decades, I said, "Yes."

"Bring her," Faith said.

"Faith, from the way they talked, strolling arm in arm, I'm sure they want to be alone," Dennis said.

Faith turned her head looked at me, and said, "Dave, you're so shy and now you've fallen in love with someone who you have to leave in two days. Don't you have more control over your emotions?"

"Let him enjoy himself," Dennis said.

We ate an Italian-American dinner, discussing the beauty of Sorrento and reminiscing about the islands we had visited. As we drank espresso, Dennis asked, "What time should we meet at the high-speed ferry to return to Naples, the day after tomorrow?"

"Early in the morning, eight o'clock," Faith replied.

"OK," Dennis said.

Again, I remained silent. Faith looked at me, "Are you coming with us?"

Since I couldn't avoid the direct question, I said, "No, I want to see more of Sorrento." They both shook their heads and said, "Dave!"

Continuing what had now become a habit I met Arabella at her store and walked her home. We visited several of the other stores, and she described the origin of their food, wine, pottery, and clothes.

As we entered the Piazza della Vittoria near my hotel, she said, "You'll miss Sorrento, when you leave in two days."

"Arabella, I've changed my original plans. I'll be staying for a few more days."

Arabella looked at me with a sensual smile that made me wish I had dated this Italian immigrant four decades ago in Brooklyn, and said, "Good, I've so much more to show you than just the ruins. When will you be leaving?"

"I don't know. I have an open return reservation."

She squeezed my arm and said, "You'll enjoy Pompeii. After we return I'll serve you a Cena, a small dinner, so we don't have to eat in a restaurant."

The drive to Pompeii reminded me of my first trip on a roller coaster. I assumed Arabella would be gentler on the curving mountain roads than the Italian taxi drivers. While I tried to suppress my fear, Arabella noticed me holding on tight to the car door handle and pressing my other hand against the dash board as she drove up and down the steep mountain roads, or made a sharp turn to avoid driving off a cliff and plunging into the Bay of Naples. She remained quiet until we reached Pompeii, and after parking asked, "Did you like the drive?"

"It's beautiful. There's nothing like this on the east coast of the U.S."

"You were quiet on the drive. Do Americans always appear rigid and hold on to the car the way you did?"

"It depends on the road."

"Dave, don't worry. You'll get used to Italian driving before you leave."

I had another reason for my lack of conversation. I wondered what I'd say if I met Faith and Dennis in the ruins.

Arabella reached into the back seat and opened a cooler to retrieve two bottles of water. "It will be hot today, we'll need these. I've packed salami sandwiches."

"I planned to take you to lunch."

"These are better than any we can buy at a restaurant."

Before we purchased tickets, I mentioned, "We used portable audio devices at Herculaneum. Should we rent them before we enter?"

"Don't be silly. I'm descended from the original residents of Pompeii who didn't die when Vesuvius erupted. I know everything about the old city."

Arabella did. She warned me to stay away from the stray dogs, prone to biting. She described each area and building with clarity and confidence. I wish I had taped our tour. It would make a great series on PBS or the Travel Channel. During her explanations, I kept looking for Faith and Dennis. Fortunately, the Pompeii ruins had a large enough area, so we missed each other. I relaxed as the tour ended, and we drove back to Sorrento. The trip back had less tension than on the trip to Pompeii, and only occasionally did I assume my rigid frightened position on the sharpest turns. As Arabella stated earlier; I w o u l d become used to Italian driving before I left Italy.

We returned to Sorrento at six. She stopped at my hotel and said, "Today, the heat exhausted me. I'm going home to take a shower and prepare the Cena. You should relax and shower, it will make you feel better. I'll see you at seven."

When I arrived, Arabella opened the door, kissed me on both cheeks and handed me a glass of Falanghina white wine. Her beauty overwhelmed me. She wore a light flowing blue dress and an aroma of lavender flowers. My mind became enchanted by her, remembering our past few days together. I wondered about our future and if I would ever leave Italy. I had heard the Sirens that tempted Ulysses lived in southern Italy. Perhaps she had descended from them. My mind returned to the present when she walked into the dining room carrying a large tray of calamari Antipasto. We talked about the trip to Pompeii. While we finished the meal with lemon gelato she asked me, "Dave, have you made plans for seeing other parts of Italy?"

"No, I plan to stay around here."

"I have to work tomorrow, but I'm sure I can get my niece to run the store the next day. We should visit Paestum, a 2,500 year old Greek city on the Mediterranean south of Salerno."

"I'd like that."

She said, "Let's do the dishes before we relax on the couch and drink our Limoncello."

As we sat on her couch, holding the iced metal glass of Limoncello, I proposed a toast, "To the most beautiful woman, greatest cook, and best tour guide in Italy."

"Why not all of Europe?"

Before I could answer, she moved in close to my face, touching my cheeks with her soft hands and tenderly kissed my lips.

Arabella woke me at seven a.m., whispering, "I wanted you to experience an authentic Italian woman, and like the lemon gelato, I hope it will make you return."

"It will." I wondered if I'd ever leave her, and if

the shrill sound I heard in the background came from a police car.

"How long will you stay at your hotel?"

"I have no commitment. It's day to day."

"Dave, it's silly for you to stay at the Regina when you're spending most of your time with me. Check out today and meet me here for the siesta with your luggage. You'll have more fun with me than staying alone."

The next ten days were heaven for this sailor. Arabella chauffeured me throughout southern Italy. Her niece ran her store every other day.

On the eleventh day, Arabella returned from work for the siesta. After we finished eating I said, "I talked to my son, Eric, earlier."

"Dave, why do you look worried?"

"Eric's concerned that I'm staying here too long."

"Did you tell him why?" Arabella stared into my eyes.

"I didn't have to. One of my sailing friends told him about you."

"Why didn't you tell him?" She sat at the table not moving her eyes from mine.

"I don't discuss my social life with my kids. After my wife died, they feared I'd fall in love with someone who'd break my heart and steal my money. When they found I dated someone they'd hound me." I tried to interpret her body language, as she sat upright and rigid at the table, her stern face and dark eyes questioning me. I wondered if my explanation changed her view of me. Fearing the worst I gripped the table with my hands.

"Does he think I'm after your money?"

"Probably. Eric's booked a flight to visit me and meet you next week." While Arabella had prepared the siesta lunch, I had neglected to clear the dirty dishes from the table, a tarnished setting for this serious conversation.

"Good, I'll be glad to meet him and show him he has nothing to fear."

Arabella moved her hand, picked up her glass of Chianti, took a sip and smiled. I listened to the chirping of thrushes at the bird feeder, and the sounds of muffled Italian being spoken on the street below while trying to interpret her expression.

"Are you sure?" My adrenaline continued to flow. Arabella obviously does not know how I live in the States, the beach house, cars, ski condo, and the size of my financial portfolio.

"Definitely."

"I'll book a room at the Hotel Regina."

"Nonsense. Eric can stay at the villa on my farm." Her face displayed a sensual smile.

"Villa? Farm?" I imagined the lemon trees, thinking she had property on the side of the mountain.

"Dave, I guess I haven't told you. A woman can't be too careful. I had to be sure you weren't dangerous and after my money."

"That sounds very American."

"I learned something by living in America. You've been drinking Limoncello made on the farm. We sell it throughout Italy and in parts of America. My dad moved to Brooklyn to open a market in the U.S."

"Why don't you live in the villa?" I thought it a waste of money for her to rent an apartment when she had a villa.

"The apartment is closer to the shop and besides I own the building."

"Why are you telling me this now?" I asked wondering what else she owned, perplexed at her withholding information from me.

"So you're not concerned about your son finding out he's right."

"Arabella, I'm not worried since you don't know whether I'm poor, middle-class, or rich."

Her sensual smile turned all knowing. "You're rich enough. Traveling to Italy, sailing for two weeks and staying for an extra two."

"Most retired middle-class Americans can do that."

"Dave, I liked the pictures of your house." Her

eyes joined the smile.

"My house?"

"Yes, I Googled you. Very impressive background." She took a sip of wine. "And I used Google maps to look at your house. It's beautiful, two-story sprawling home on an acre of land in Henlopen boarding the Rehoboth–Lewes canal. I like your blue Lexus sports convertible more than the SUV."

"What else do you know?" I asked wondering whether I should feel violated or jealous because she had examined my background. Meanwhile I had assumed she was a middle-class owner of a gelato store. Her explanation did not reduce my stress, only changed its nature from fear of my son's behavior to that of losing her.

"Well. You're not an ex-convict and don't abuse women. I asked the *Been Verified* website for a complete report."

"Really! When did you do this?"

"The second night after we met, and you walked me part of the way home."

I remembered the salty air of the sea breeze, and my first experience with the fragrance of the lemon trees in the mountains and our conversation to learn about and impress each other.

"That early?"

"Dave, I wanted to make sure you wouldn't

attack me during lunch. Thanks for not trying to seduce me with stories of your wealth. I liked that."

"Arabella, you seduced me first."

The tension drained from my body, and I smiled remembering her kiss.

"Only your body. Your mind took longer."

Thinking about my affection for Arabella for the past weeks, and realizing our conversation shattered my self-control, I said, "Arabella, I love you."

"No man can resist my lemon gelato."

"Arabella, it's more than your dessert."

"Dave, I feel the same way, that's why I seduced your body and invited you to stay with me so I could work on your mind."

I wondered why men are the last to realize what's happening to them. Well, my son will be happy.

My First Psych Course

At eighteen, in the 1960s, I shared many psychological traits with my contemporaries. I had left my religion and began searching for an alternative explanation for life.

I enrolled at Hofstra University near my home in Long Island, New York to pursue the social sciences. My courses included economics, psychology, and the normal required liberal arts courses: English, history, and chemistry. While most of my courses went well, taught by knowledgeable and humorous instructors, Introduction to Psychology 101 left the most lasting impression.

Phase 1 – Psychology 101

The Psych 101 course had three sections. I enrolled in the Monday – Wednesday – Friday 11:00 a.m. class, rather than the Tuesday – Thursday daytime or evening classes. After purchasing the required texts I felt a little foreboding about the course since our section had two books assigned while the others only had one, an introductory text, *Psychology and Life*, fifth edition by Floyd L. Ruch. It measured eight and one-half inches by ten inches, filled with easy-to-understand graphics and photos. The other assigned book included an ominous olive green cover, six inch by eight and one-half inch thick book devoid of color and graphics, *Principles of Psychology*, by Fred S. Keller and William N. Schoeonfeld.

Class 1

The first class of over ninety students started out well. Lecturer Bradley Walk introduced himself and outlined the course. Later I discovered that a lecturer isn't a professor. They haven't received their Ph.D., earn a low salary, posses no teaching skills, and devote most of their time working on their Ph.D. dissertation.

Walk ended the first hourly class a half hour early by giving us a reading assignment. "For Wednesday, please read Chapter 1 'Man Studies Himself' from *Psychology and Life* (the authors of the book were not aware the sexual revolution had started) and Chapter 1 'Psychology and the Reflex' in the *Principles of Psychology* text." While lecturer Walk talked, my eyes wandered and I noticed a blond girl who caught my glance and smiled at me. After class, I coolly tried to walk over to her, only to find she had disappeared, presumably to go to another class since her smile told me she didn't want to avoid me.

Class 2

Excited by a return to learning and visions of the blond, I read both assignments. *Psychology and Life* presented an interesting, easy to understand history of psychology and psychological concepts, ending with a discussion on the scientific techniques of psychology.

The second reading confused me compared to the informative first book. Written in a highly formalized academic style, this book defined psychology in abstract terms as the science of explaining the behavior of any life form. My economics professor might have contested this assertion since he taught economically motivated behavior. The text asserted that the study of the environment, stimulus, and response behavior were critical concepts in psychology. I accepted these claims on faith, noting the dichotomy between the two texts.

The class began by lecturer Walk cautioning, "Everyone should do the assigned reading since this material will be on the departmental test for the three sections of this class."

I heeded this warning since I wanted to pass.

Especially since he only spent ten minutes summarizing the *Psychology and Life* chapter and the remaining forty minutes on the *Principles of Psychology* reading.

Walk spoke in a drab monotone during the first discussion, but switched to emitting excited sounds and showing his delight when describing the reflex, the response mechanism, the reflex arc, reflex properties, the threshold or the limen, latency, stimulus intensity and response magnitude, and reflex strength. Walk's excitable diction baffled the students even those who had completed the reading. I couldn't understand why Walk didn't spend more time talking about the elementary concepts in *Psychology and Life* to introduce the beginning students to topics they could comprehend.

At the end of the class he assigned the first section of Chapter 2 "Heredity and Maturation" from the *Psychology and Life* book and Chapter 2 "Respondent Conditioning" from the drab olive book.

I glimpsed at the blond leaving class when the lecture ended. During the first class, I noticed she had a beautiful face, but now I glanced at her athletic body and decided I had to meet her.

Hoping not to look like a stalker, I followed her and found her sitting alone in the cafeteria eating a brown bag sandwich and reading. After going to the food line and buying a hamburger and fries, I sat across from her and asked, "What do you think of the Psych class?"

She looked up, surprise on her face, and said, "Strange." I assumed she referred to the class.

I couldn't tell from her short answer if I overwhelmed her emotionally, but I continued. "I'm John."

"I'm Rebecca, but everyone calls me Becky," she replied.

"Walk is a strange character. Notice how the first readings from *Psychology and Life* bored him, but he acted like a kid who had been told to eat as much candy as he wanted, when he blabbed about the psycho terms from the olive green book. Most of the students didn't understand his lecture."

"I did the reading and understood, didn't you?"she replied.

Humbled, I acknowledged, "Yes I understood them since I did the reading, but most of the class didn't."

Becky smiled when I told her I read the assignment, and said, "I have to read it, since I'm a pre-med student and have to get an A in any course related to the body. What's your major?"

"I'm only a freshman, I haven't decided."

"So you're uncertain about your future?" she asked.

"True. I recognize the importance of Walk's statement to read the other book even if his lectures aren't based on it."

"So do I. I have a friend in the Tuesday and Thursday day section. I'll ask her if they're being taught the same material as our class," she replied.

"Let me know. It could help us prepare for our tests. While I'm not a pre-med student, I too want to get an A."

At that point in the conversation, I noticed she had finished her sandwich and picked up her books, saying, "I have to go to the library and get ready for my next class. See you later."

I didn't take offense that she left while I had not finished eating since I admired her drive to become a doctor and her need to study.

Class 3

The third class, held on Friday, replicated the second. Mr. Walk spent ten minutes reviewing the assignment in *Psychology and Life* and devoted the remainder of the class to Chapter 2 "Respondent Conditioning" in *Principles of Psychology*. He appeared to be approaching a state of ecstasy as he described the work of Pavlov. Walk showed a movie of the old man, pictured ringing a bell, and the dogs responding on cue by salivating. I couldn't see the significance of this experiment since I r e m e m b e r e d salivating as a toddler when my mother rang the dinner bell. I still become excited when I glance at my watch and realize it's lunch time.

When the class ended, he assigned the last two sections of Chapter 2 "Heredity and Maturation" from the *Psychology and Life* book and Chapter 3 "Operant Conditioning" from the drab olive book. I soon discovered the olive book had earned the students' ranking as the most boring textbook of their college careers.

Becky sat in the front of the class, but since I had to work that afternoon parking cars at a golf course, I couldn't eat lunch with her. I left without speaking to her so I'd arrive on time for work.

Class 4

The Monday class returned to the form of Friday's class with Mr. Walk using the first ten minutes reviewing the assignment in *Psychology and Life* and excitedly explained Chapter 3 "Operant Conditioning" in *Principles of Psychology*. Mr. Walk appeared to beam as he stated that unlike respondent conditioning, operant conditioning could be used to train organisms. He did not use the words *men, women or children*, but wanted to keep the principles abstract and general. Walk showed movies of pigeons and rats being conditioned to perform a specific task for food. I wondered why these experiments excited

Mr. Walk since I learned in my first classes in economics that money motivated behavior, and food played the role of money in the film.

True to the tradition of the first three classes Walk continued assigning reading material: Chapter 3 "Measurement of Individual and Group Differences" in *Psychology and Life* and Chapter 4 "Extinction and Reconditioning" in the other text.

I had lunch with Becky after class. She surprised me as I sat across from her with an Italian sub and coke on my tray, when she said, "I missed you on Friday. I thought you found a better lunch companion."

"No chance of that. I had to work. I park cars at a golf course in Rockville Centre on Friday afternoon and the weekends."

"You're not rich."

"No, not yet. That's why I'm going to college. Someone has to pay my tuition."

Becky smiled, saying "It's good to have ambitions. I talked to my friend in the Thursday psych section. I had planned to tell you on Friday, but today will do. She said she has a great instructor. He tells jokes during class related to the *Psychological and Life* text and hasn't mentioned the other book."

"Your friend probably looks forward to class, while we dread listening to Bradley Walk or as I have described him to my roommates, Babbling Talk."

"That's good! You have a sense of humor. However, we have to keep reading the *Psychology and Life* text since she told me her professor said the departmental test will cover the regular textbook and not the *Principles* book."

"That's great news, but I wonder will reading the text give us enough information to earn an "A" since we're missing her professor's ideas," I replied.

"I told her the same thing. She offered to let me read her class notes. If you're nice, I'll let you study them, too."

Suddenly, I realized this beautiful, athletic blond had offered to spend the rest of this semester studying Psych 101 with me. I stammered, trying to hide my joy, "Thanks, I'll be nice," wondering what she meant by 'being nice'.

"I had to swear I'd never lend the notes to anyone besides you. Since the grades are based on a curve, she doesn't want to help anyone else, because it might lower her grade. We'll have to read the notes together. She wants them back the day she gives them to us."

"I won't tell anyone else," I promised, understanding I'd see Becky at least twice a week. Who knew college could be such fun.

To my surprise, we continued talking through lunch until we had to leave for our Monday one o'clock classes.

Class 5

Our Wednesday class repeated the format of the other classes: ten minutes on *Psychology and Life* and the rest on reinforcing the behavior of pigeons and rats, illustrated via their filmed behavior.

After class, I ate lunch with Becky. While sipping her coke with a straw, she smiled and fluttered her eyes and asked, "Where did you go to high school?"

"St. Agnes in Rockville Centre."

"Too bad my parents won't let me date Catholics."

"That's okay. I've given up the faith."

"They only want me to date Jewish boys."

"Are you still a practicing Jew?"

"No, but my parents' think I am."

"Let's not tell your parents."

"Okay. Do you have a car?"

"Yes."

"It will work out then."

Not being a master of psychology but a helpless male, I didn't realize our conversation after the fifth psych class ended my career as a college bachelor.

We studied Psych 101 together and began dating. I admit she motivated me to work hard in my other courses since I believed she had more interest in my mind than my other attributes. All the Psych 101 classes we attended followed similar patterns until the first test.

The Test

Becky and I took the test on a Monday after a third of the semester ended. As her girlfriend told us, it only included questions from the *Psychology and Life* book. After the test, we both agree we'd aced it. Our grades delivered on Friday verified this result. Unfortunately, many of our classmates failed or received "D" grades since they concentrated on studying their lecture notes and the *Principles* book.

Phase 2 – Psychology 101

Class 1

Becky and I never saw Mr. Babble Talk again. Instead, the Psychology Department Chairman, Professor Warren Ives, in his mid-fifties, bald and forty pounds overweight, addressed the class on the Monday after we received our test grades, saying he would teach the course for the rest of the semester. Ives' explanation of why he replaced Mr. Walk did not please many of the students.

Professor Ives formally addressed us, "I want to thank this class for participating in an educational psychology experiment which Mr. Walk managed as part of his Ph.D. dissertation. He taught a second level course in this class to test whether teaching advanced concepts is better for the students than presenting watered-down introductory course material. The test results will either validate or disprove his hypothesis."

Our silent reaction unnerved Professor Ives, who as a lover of psychology expected the students to be thrilled at being part of an experiment. He didn't foresee what happened next. A few students stood up and left the class in silence. We later learned they walked straight to the Dean of Liberal Arts and complained about instructor Walk, the content of the test, and unknowingly being made part of an experiment when they had paid for an education and not to test a stupid hypothesis.

After those students left, others expressed their objections to the college's treatment of them complaining about the unfairness of the test and its impact on their final grade. Professor Ives suddenly understood their objections and said, "The results of the test will not be part of the final grade, unless you did well."

Ives' statement quieted the students and he taught the material from Chapter 4 "Intelligence and Other Human Abilities" from the *Psychology and Life* book. He never mentioned the drab olive book again.

We later heard the Dean had pacified the students by agreeing with them, stating he hadn't approved of the experiment, and he would forbid future experiments unless the students agreed to participate. It would have been interesting to hear the Dean's discussion with Professor Ives.

At lunch Becky and I, at first irate at what we heard about the class experiment eventually realized since we did well in the course, it wouldn't harm our academic careers.

"Do you like our new professor?" I asked Becky.

"He's kind of sleazy. Did you see how he looked at some of the girls?"

"No." Why did I miss this type of behavior that Becky observed?

"Well, pay attention next class. It's hard to miss."

Class 2

Professor Ives stuck to the assigned Chapter 4 from the *Psychology and Life* text. His gave clear and concise lectures, using a slide projector to present material not in the book to emphasize his points. He never exposed us to old movies of pigeons and rats.

Ives stated we would learn more if we asked him questions and that he always queried the students to validate they understood his lectures. A male asked first. Professor Ives responded by saying, "Please state your name, so we'd get to know each other." No one ever asked anything in Babble Talk's classes.

A young girl in a short skirt and tight sweater asked the next question. Professor Ives' reaction validated Becky's assertion of him as a dirty old man. He beamed when she raised her hand and stated her name which he wrote down. She asked her question which he answered, but Ives asked her a question at the end of his answer. This dialogue continued for several minutes. At the end of the exchange, he asked the class, "Do you recognize what I just did?"

Several of the women quietly smiled while most of the men had no clue. He answered his own question. "The exchange of questions and answers mirrors the teaching processes Socrates used in ancient Greece."

That's a fancy name for flirting with a female student, I thought.

Ives spent at least three times longer in his discussions with the female students than with the males, always writing the names of the female students in his notes and only occasionally noting a male's name.

After class, Becky and I shared our traditional lunch.

"You're right; he is a sleaze, the way he talked to the women compared to the men," I said.

"Women have a sixth sense about men like the

professor. They need it to survive. Did you see how many of the women dressed, as sexy as possible without looking like sluts? We never dressed that way for Babble Talk."

"I never look at other women."

"Right. I saw you staring. It's only natural."

"I guess they dressed sexier than usual. Actually, you're pretty alluring today."

"Girls who recognize his behavior dress that way, knowing he'll notice and that will improve their grades."

"You're kidding!" Why didn't I recognize this grade-motivated behavior?

Additional Classes

Professor Ives continued to expand the concepts in the book via slide presentations. However, his Socratic flirting with the female students became more blatant with each class.

In a class on emotions and disease, we learned of Professor Ives' claim to fame. He stated he had published many academic articles, advocating that grape seeds and not emotional problems caused ulcers. I wondered about the significance of his research because most people eat seedless grapes. Ives published his research decades before 1982 when Australian scientists Barry Marshall and Robin Warren found and conclusively demonstrated that

Helicobacter pylori bacteria caused the vast majority of ulcers.

Paradoxically, the more sexist he became, the more he acted as if the female students liked him. They didn't. Ives tried to ask young women embarrassing questions during our discussion of human sexuality. I'll never forget his last question addressed to a young shapely redhead, dressed in a tight red sweater who became the repeated object of his Socratic flirting.

"Marilyn Simpkins, you're young and attractive and must think about sex all the time. What is a stronger physical drive: sex or thirst?"

"Well, Professor Ives. It depends. If I satisfy my thirst with enough alcohol, I might imagine sex with you, about how disgusting it would be."

The class howled. Professor Ives's face became red. He started shaking and fell on his face.

We were shocked. A student stood up and rushed forward and saw him turning blue. She yelled, "I'm a nurse, someone call the college infirmary and ask for an ambulance. Tell whoever answers that he just collapsed, and he may have had a stroke or heart attack." Five students raced from the room and made the calls.

The nurse applied CPR to the body without a response. The ambulance arrived within ten minutes, and the Emergency Medical Technician took over from the nurse. Within a few minutes, he declared, "There's nothing we can do for him."

The students who had been milling in the classroom left after the EMT's announcement.

At lunch, Becky and I discussed his sudden death. She spoke first, "While a good teacher, I despised his behavior toward women. Too bad he died."

"He could teach, but he didn't take care of himself. I've seen him outside of class smoking. Ives looked like he must have overeaten every night. I'm glad you exercise, I caddy, and we don't smoke, and have healthy eating habits."

"True, but we're in the minority. I wonder what will happen for the rest of the semester."

We had a normal individual for the third professor of my first semester psych course. He apologized for our earlier treatment, and did his best to prepare us for the department-wide "Introduction to Psychology" test. Both Becky and I earned A grades. We skipped the second semester Psych 102 until we learned more about the psychology professors.

Phase 3 - Psychology 102

Becky and I were pleasantly surprised when we attended the first class of Psych 102 a year later. A beautiful blond woman, in her thirties, stood in front of the class.

"I'm Professor Mary O'Malley and I'll be your instructor for this semester."

She had a stellar reputation as a teacher. I noticed the male students leaned forward and stared at the new professor, not wanting to miss a word as they examined her body. Becky also noticed and moved her head next to mine and whispered, "Mister, remember you're taken."

I hated that she could read my mind. I replied, "Happily taken."

Professor O'Malley competently presented an outline for the semester, and then told us why she had become a psychologist.

"I grew up in a strict Catholic family, attended Catholic School and experienced the nuns."

Many of the class nodded about their shared experience, but weren't prepared for her next words.

"My family and the nuns traumatized me so much about the sinfulness of sex; the fear of sex obsessed me. As a young child, I didn't understand the natural development of the body and the sex drive since my parents avoided talking about that subject. As I hit puberty, and my body changed, my periods began and attractions for boys started, I knew I committed continuous mortal sins that would condemn me to hell forever. I had such great aversion to these feelings that I reversed my consciousness. My mind tricked me into believing my wakeful periods were my dreams and my dreams, my conscious life."

The class became silent. Professor O'Malley continued, "As I became older this phase passed but I'll never forgot it. I became a psychologist to study if this behavior was normal."

Becky looked at me and whispered, "Here we go again."

My First Car

The Lexus dealer handed me the keys to a silver 2009 SC 430 hardtop convertible after I gave him a check for $72,532. I had come a long way from being a caddy and parking lot attendant at a golf course in Rockville Centre, New York where those menial jobs had financed my college education. After putting the top down I drove to our five thousand square foot, five-bedroom summer beach house in Southampton, New York. My daughter Judy and my grandson planned to visit me in two days. I couldn't wait to show him the car.

Judy arrived while I ate breakfast on the patio with my wife, who said after we finished eating, "I'm going to play tennis. Have a good time with Stan." I walked to the pool on the side of the house where my seven year old grandson Stan waded at the shallow end.

"Hi granddad. You have a new car!"

"Do you want to take a ride?"

"Yeah."

"Follow me." We walked to the car parked in the circular driveway in front of the house, and I put Stan in the back seat.

"Can't I sit in the front seat?"

"No, you know you can't. Wait a few years until you're older." Stan weighed fifty pounds and at four feet tall, had a long wait. After strapping him in, I walked to the driver's side.

Judy, who resembled her mother, brown hair, thin, and medium height walked up and asked, "Can I go too?"

Without waiting for an answer she opened the door, sat in the passenger's seat, and fastened the seat belt. I did the same, and then released the latches securing the solid top and pressed the button to raise it. I looked at my grandson whose eyes grew large as the mechanism started, lowering the windows, raising the solid metal roof and lowering it into the trunk. His head followed the top and his mouth, for a change, did not open. Finally he exclaimed, "Wow!"

After starting the car, I drove through the gate bordered by fifteen-foot hedges that surrounded the two-acre lot, typical of most homes in Southampton.

"Stan, your granddad loves convertibles. Did you know when a member of the Mafia they helped him get his first convertible, a blue and white 1958

Chevy?" Judy said as we pulled into the street. I took a left turn and drove to the beach.

Stan's eyes widened again having seen enough TV to recognize the Mafia as an evil organization. He knew no one left the Mafia unless they were killed or died. Stan said disapprovingly, "Granddad you're in the Mafia?"

"No. Judy, why do you say those things about me? Stan, if your mother tells you outlandish stories, check with me before you believe them," I watched my daughter smile as I spoke.

"Yes, granddad."

"Are you going to tell him about your first car?" Judy asked.

"Of course. I wasn't in the Mafia, but worked for a guy in the Mafia and didn't realize it for at least a year. I parked cars at a golf course in New York. After working for six months, my boss Tony asked, 'I have an opening in my Sunday newspaper delivery business. Do you want the job? It pays $20 besides what you make parking cars during the day.'" I drove slowly in the congested streets as I talked.

"You weren't in the Mafia?" my grandson asked, looking at his mother.

"No, but I accepted Tony's offer, 'Sure. How early?'" I asked.

"'Meet me inside this warehouse at 4 a.m.'

He handed me a paper with the address.

"That's early.

"'You're being paid $20 because it's early,' a fortune in 1966, so I agreed. After three months delivering the Sunday papers, I heard rumors from the other employees that Tony worked for the Mafia. In those days, the mob controlled parking, newspaper deliveries, loan sharking, drugs, construction, and many unions. I ignored the rumors until I met Tony's brother, Marco.

"The parking lot attendants worked in a small grey wooden ten by ten foot building. It had four chairs and a small table. An electric space heater provided warmth in the winter. In the summer, we kept the door open to keep the temperatures below one hundred degrees.

"Marco used to visit Tony and talk to me and the other parking lot attendants. He told funny stories of his experiences in the Army, knowing we were worried about being drafted and sent to Vietnam. Marco would ask if we were doing well in college, and if we had future career plans.

"I told him as a sophomore, I hadn't decided what to do, but wanted to get rich. A mistake.

"After a few months, he came to the parking lot only when I worked. Marco confirmed my suspicions that he and his brother had Mafia connections when one day he walked into our attendants' building, sat on a chair and said, 'I've started a new business. I've just returned from Canada. I'm in the import business. The goods are in the car trunk.'

"Marco had mentioned being in construction, a bartender and a list of other manual jobs. I asked him what he imported.

"Marco gave me a serious look and said, 'Things.' The look told me not to inquire further. While polite to him over the next few months, I became cautious when he invited me to join him and Tony for a beer. I usually declined citing studying for exams or having a date. When I joined them they were perfect gentlemen, but I felt they wanted to recruit me to be their accountant after I earned my business degree.

"In my junior year at Hofstra, I used my father's second car, a 1958 Packard four-door green sedan to deliver papers. It froze from an oil leak on Sunday morning after I had finished the paper route. Marco used this opportunity to ingratiate himself. He came to the attendants' shack on Monday morning and said, 'I heard your car died. How did you get here from Flushing?'

"A ride lasting an hour on two buses. I changed at the Hempstead station.

"'I can solve your problem and help you get a car,' Marco offered.

"How?"

"'I have friends in Brooklyn.'

"How can they help?

"'They sold me a car. What type of car do you want?

"Something cheap, a convertible. I can only afford three hundred.

"'Let me talk to my friends and see what they can do. I'll try and get one Thursday or Friday so you can deliver papers on Sunday.'

"On Wednesday morning, Marco returned and said, 'My friends called, they have a car that's perfect, a blue, eight year old Chevy convertible. You'll love it.'

"How much?

"'Two hundred and seventy-five. Bring an extra twenty-five for the license plates and registration.'

"When can I see it? Are they going to bring it here?

"'No. You have to go to them. I've set it up. On Thursday, go to the corner of Fulton Street and Hudson Avenue, in Brooklyn across from the Department of Motor Vehicles. Just stand on the corner. Be there by ten. A friend of mine, Sam, a big guy will introduce himself and show you the car.'

"How will I recognize him?

"'You won't. But he'll know you.' I had learned not to ask questions.

"'If you want it, buy it; if not, no hard feelings.

Bring cash for the car and the registration, three hundred, no checks.'

"On Thursday, I arrived at the designated corner at nine-thirty and went into a Chock Full O' Nuts Coffee Shop, had coffee, a donut, and read the newspaper. At five to ten, I left the shop and walked to the corner and waited.

"At ten, a large Italian, six feet two, weighing over two hundred and forty, in his mid-twenties, with several scars on his face and arms, dressed in dark blue slacks and a black short sleeve shirt approached and asked, 'Are you Steve?'

"Yes, Sam?" I felt relieved he was Marco's friend since this guy could hurt me. I wondered if Sam worked as a soldier in the Mafia, collecting bad debts and killing on command, when not selling cars.

"He said, 'Marco gave me a good description of you. Let me show you the car.'

"We walked down Fulton Street and turned into Rockwell Place.

"'Here she is. Has a few dents but works great. Get in. Let's go for a drive,' Sam said.

"Sam gave me the keys. I drove around the block, returning to the same parking space.

"'If you want it, give me two seventy-five and I'll give you the bill of sale and the registration.'

"Fine, I'll take it. It cost four hundred or more

on used car lots.

"I gave Sam the cash.

"'Get the car registered at the Department of Motor Vehicles on the corner. Just go into the building. The windows for vehicle registration are on your right. Go to the line on the far left. There should be a woman in a brown dress, an older lady with bleached-blond curly hair. Give her the sales receipt, the old registration, the filled out new registration form, and twenty-five dollars, and ask to have the car registered. You can't miss her.'

"What if she's not there?

"'Don't go to that or any other window. Leave and I'll be here. If she's there, just smile when you leave. I'll see you. If you or your friends need anything else just tell Marco or Tony.'

"'I'll do that. Thanks.

"Sam gave me the keys, and as I walked to the Department of Motor Vehicles, I looked at the bill of sale and the registration. The names on both documents were identical, but the signatures differed. When Marco first proposed the sale, I thought he might sell me a stolen car. Now I knew it. A queasy feeling settled over me. I broke into a cold sweat but kept moving. I feared offending a car thief with connections, and took the risk of being arrested for trying to register a stolen car. I couldn't back out, since I suspected I'd lose the money, and needed a car. If Sam belonged to Marco's organization, I reasoned, the registration should have no problems. My stomach soon settled. I went to the window of the curly-haired blond and registered the car as planned.

"The woman didn't look at me and said, 'That'll be twenty-five.' I gave her the money. She handed me the new registration document and the plates.

"As I left the Department of Motor Vehicles smiling, I saw Sam and waved. Sam acknowledged me by nodding his head and left. I kept the car for six years through college and law school and never joined the Mafia."

We had arrived at the beach. My grandson didn't speak until I finished parking. Then he asked, "Granddad, so you never killed anyone."

"Did your mother say I did?"

"She said to ask you when I asked her."

"No, but maybe I should have."

My First July 4 Rehoboth Beach Weekend

John Simmons invited me to join him at his singles group Dewey Beach house on a July 4 weekend several decades ago. "Steve, the trip will end your depression," John said.

"John, I'm not depressed, but I'll go since I've heard so much about the beach."

"Don't kid yourself. Everyone's miserable after a divorce. If you can't return to normal after a July 4th weekend at the beach, you're a candidate to live the rest of your days moping around."

"I said I'll go. Please don't feel sorry for me. I don't need you, or anyone else to be my psychiatrist."

John, wise in the ways of those who had helped other friends recover from divorce, smiled but did not reply. Since July 4 occurred on a Saturday that year, we left early Friday afternoon to avoid the traffic. I grew up on Long Island, New York and had frequented Long Beach and Jones Beach and visited the Hamptons as a teenager. However, I didn't know what to expect on my first singles weekend in Delaware.

John described his beach house as an old ten-room farmhouse on the exotically named New Orleans Avenue. I had visualized an English Tudor style house on a two-acre estate surrounded by fifteen foot hedges, entered through a gate on a circular driveway: The actual house would not have passed zoning in Southampton. The house had two stories with clapboard siding covered in fading light yellow paint. A full length porch on the front of the house appeared less than ten feet from the road. It had seven bedrooms, but the three on the first floor could fit within my condo bedroom.

After we unloaded the car and I chose a single bedroom on the first floor, I confronted John in the kitchen. He leaned against the stove sipping a beer.

"Want one?" he reached into the fridge and handed me a beer.

I struggled to keep my cool as I chugged half the beer, hoping to reduce my anger.

"Do you like the house?" he asked.

"It's not the house you described."

"Yes, it is. A seven-bedroom farmhouse."

"John, I assumed it would be on a farm with

land surrounding it."

"Steve, I forgot to tell you someone moved the house from a farm in Milton."

"My image differs from your reality. Are you sure you'll introduce me to an attractive woman as you promised? None would be caught dead in this house."

"Nonsense, they all want to be invited to our gourmet dinners at our rustic house."

I didn't ask him for a typical menu. At this house I assumed they served franks and beans.

"Don't look at me as if you want to be somewhere else. Let's go for a run, and I'll show you the beauty of the inland bays and the ocean. Tonight we'll go dancing in Rehoboth, and I'll take you on a tour of the high-class neighborhoods where the women you'll meet live. You'll forget our rustic beach house."

Not wanting to assume the weekend would get worse, I consented. Dressed in shorts, t-shirts and running shoes, we ran from our house to Route 1 and proceeded south on the right side of the road south. As we left the last houses in Dewey Beach, the view of the inland bays and the ocean sand dunes improved my mental state. John explained the World War II role of the deserted towers on our left. While running, I took in the beauty of the scenery, realizing John's verbalizations were his attempt at lifting me from my revulsion at the beach house.

After we passed Keybox Road, I noticed two women at least a half mile away running toward us, both wearing white shorts. As we approached their formless bodies, one turned into a blond in a ponytail, two inches shorter than me with curves that her pale blue sweat shirt could not hide. The other woman, tall and thin, wore a gray t-shirt, and had red hair cut in an Irish version of an Afro style from the 1960s.

John said, "The women are healthier at the beach. Most run, play tennis or dance to keep thin."

"They're running faster than we are. Are they your friends?" I asked.

"No, but don't fall for the first woman you meet. That's how recently divorced men get in trouble and remarry within a year to someone they'll divorce a few years later."

We stopped talking when they were within twenty yards. As they crossed our path they smiled and the red head said, "Good afternoon."

The blond said, "Great day for a run."

Being non-creative males we said "Hi."

"Are they attractive to you?" John asked.

"Hard to tell. They're in great shape and look good in their athletic garb. I wonder how they look dressed up."

"I agree. There's a chance you'll never see them

again, or you might meet them tonight. They look our age so they'll probably go to Fran O'Brien's in Rehoboth to dance and meet men."

"Is that where we're going?"

"Yes, and if they don't show up, there will be plenty of other women you can try your lines on."

"I don't use lines."

"Yes you do, but you're unaware you use them. Try to be simple, they'll recognize if you're acting to impress them. My best approach is to say 'Hi, I'm John,' or 'Do you want to dance?'"

"I'll try."

When we returned to the house, I met two of the beach house members who had arrived during our run: Betsy and George. I assumed they were a couple, but soon learned they had arrived separately. Betsy introduced herself by describing her job as most Washingtonians do when meeting someone. At thirty-three and divorced, her intellect and her slender tanned body and wind tossed black hair impressed me. Her face reminded me of Natalie Wood. Betsy held a master's degree from Carnegie Mellon University and worked as a statistician at the National Institutes of Health in Bethesda. George in his early forties, quieter than Betsy, earned an accounting degree from the University of Maryland and worked for a private government contractor.

After sharing dinner of takeout pizza, the four of

us went to Rehoboth. They introduced me to their summer social world. After impressing me with their tour, they assured me that our final stop at Fran O'Brien's would excite and convince me Rehoboth Beach was the ideal location for a recently divorced man to spend the summer.

We entered the bar and walked the short hallway, flanked by entrances to the men's and women's rooms on the right, toward an open area facing a long bar half filled with patrons. Betsy turned right toward the twenty-by-fifteen-foot dance floor and found a four-person table. Adults ranging in age from the late twenties to the sixties danced to the sounds of *Life in the Fast Lane* by the Eagles.

Betsy and I danced to *This Old Heart of Mine* by the Isley Brothers before she became inundated with invitations from her male beach friends. After finishing my first beer, I left the table and wandered to the bar and ordered another. When I tried to return to the table, a group watching the dancers blocked me. Rather than disturb them during the song, I stood and watched the sensual bodies of the women sway to the music. After the song ended, a beautiful woman with long blond hair falling off her bare shoulders, standing next to me said, "We had a perfect day for an afternoon run."

Astounded, as a depressed divorced man according to John, at this angelic woman addressing me, I stammered, "Yes, I enjoyed it. Did you see me run today?"

"I ran right past you."

Not understanding, I looked at her, without speaking.

"You don't recognize me. I look different now. I had a pony tail and wore a blue sweat shirt and white shorts. My name's Shari."

My face sported an involuntary smile, "I remember. It's my first time at the beach. I'm Steve."

She smiled. "I see your running friend has found mine. They're dancing on the other side of the dance floor."

I realized I had been staring at her when I found it difficult to move my head and look at John and his red-headed partner.

"Her name is Anne. Do you dance?"

"Yes." I took her hand, and we moved onto the dance floor, performing a slow swing to *Brown Eyed Girl* by Van Morrison. We talked and danced the next four songs. Between the dances, I learned she taught economics at the University of Maryland, which I thought more impressive than being a lawyer. She moved from Ohio to Chevy Chase, Maryland and loved the Washington DC area. She had a membership in a beach house in Henlopen Acres. When I described my background she listened attentively, but smiled warmly when I told her I lived in the Van Ness complex on Connecticut Avenue, a few miles from her home. Later I learned you have to live close to your partner to develop and maintain a relationship in the large Washington, DC region.

An hour after meeting Shari, she introduced me to Anne whose time John had monopolized. The DJ played *You've Lost that Lovin' Feelin'* by the Righteous Brothers. Shari and I danced to the sensual music. At the end of the dance, Shari handed me a card, "Anne and I have to leave. We're having a party at our house tomorrow night from 6 to 8, and we have to get the house ready and set up for the party."

I looked at the card, confirming the invitation, and said, "I'll be there. I enjoyed meeting and dancing with you."

"Me too. See you tomorrow night."

As I walked to our table, I read the details of the card: Dress: Beach informal; By Invitation Only; Please Bring the Invitation to the Party. I hoped John received an invitation since I had promised Shari I'd attend.

Betsy drove us home after a few more songs. After arriving, John opened a beer, handed me one and asked, "Steve, what do you think of Fran's?"

"I enjoyed it."

"You didn't take full advantage of the bar. You

only talked to one woman."

"I talked to Shari and Betsy."

"Betsy doesn't count. She's in the beach house." I wondered what he meant. Betsy looked more attractive than Shari.

"Steve, are you going to Anne and Shari's party tomorrow night?"

"Yes. I guess you're invited. What about the others in the house? It says invitation only. Will it upset them not being invited?" I replied.

"No. They'll find something to do. The party's over at eight, so we can meet them later."

"What does Dress: Beach Casual mean?" I asked.

"Just like we're dressed now. No suits or tuxes."

Waking up at 8:00 a.m. in the cramped six-by-twelve foot bedroom, refreshed from the evening of dancing and meeting beautiful women, I looked forward to my first Rehoboth Beach party. Perhaps I could enjoy the beach. I still could not imagine inviting an attractive woman, whom I wanted to date to John's beach house.

I had to admit the female beach house members of his house made me forget my ex-wife. Two brunettes, Amy and Joan, had arrived late at night. I met them during a breakfast of bacon and scrambled eggs, with cheese and vegetables, prepared by Betsy.

As the only man at the table, the women

bombarded me with questions. The other men still slept. Betsy, who after the first dance ignored me last night, acted as sweet and attentive as any woman I had talked to since my divorce. I almost forgot about Shari.

John arrived after I finished eating and fixed a bowl of Cheerios with sliced bananas on top. As he ate he caught me staring at Betsy. After he finished eating, he said, "Steve let's take a walk. I want to show you Dewey Beach in the daytime."

We left the house and walked east toward Route 1 and the ocean.

"Has your opinion of the beach house changed?" John asked.

"It's beginning to."

"Do you like the women in the house?"

"They're attractive and have interesting backgrounds and professions."

"You like Betsy?" John said.

"Yes."

"Keep it that way. Don't act on your attraction."

"What do you mean?"

"It's an unwritten rule: never date a beach house member. If a breakup occurs during the summer the house disintegrates, forming two camps backing either the man or the woman."

"That's okay. I'm not sure she likes me. Besides, I'm not a beach house member."

"You might be. There's an opening in the house. One of our members had an unexpected job transfer. If you have a good time this weekend and you don't offend the members by chasing after Betsy or someone else, you may be invited to join."

John's statement shocked me. I had too much to do in DC to waste time at the beach, including tennis, running on the C&O canal, Wolf Trap, dancing and attending activities designed to bring divorced men and women together. Although I had to admit I'd been too apprehensive to extend my feelings to those women I met in Washington. I had to decide how to refuse his offer without offending him.

John kept the pressure on, "Have you forgotten Shari? You're still going to her party tonight?"

"Yes."

"Be careful. If you go after two, you'll get the reputation as a player and get none."

I didn't understand his mental process. Yesterday when we drove to the beach he told me the weekend would cure my post-divorce depression. Now he warned me against getting a reputation for womanizing. If I did, it would not be because of my skills with women.

After returning to the house, several of us drove to Henlopen High School in Lewes to play tennis.

We met others from different beach houses and played doubles for two hours returning to the house by 11:30 a.m.

I enjoyed showering outside, appreciating the fresh-air setting, and realized while shaving the small mirror attached to the shower wall had not steamed up as it would in an indoor bathroom. The breeze in the shower refreshed me.

Unlike breakfast, we prepared our own lunch. We each made sandwiches or salads of our choosing. I had a roast beef and provolone, with mayonnaise on rye. The variety and freshness of the food in the refrigerator and pantry impressed me. "Does the house always have this much food?" I asked John.

"We try to plan our meals during the week, and someone shops on Friday when they arrive. The house runs like a commune, everyone has a task, some shop, others cook and the rest clean."

"That's amazing."

"George went shopping when we ran yesterday. It makes the house run efficiently and keeps the peace. Please don't cause friction."

"John, I get it. I won't hit on Betsy." As if I knew how. Since John's lecture, Betsy had become more desirable in my mind. Nothing like the lure of forbidden fruit. Since I didn't plan to join the house, I avoided her on the weekend, but planned to call her on Wednesday. Not having dated women for six months after my divorce, I now had to choose between two.

That afternoon four of us, Betsy, George, John and I sat at one of the picnic tables on the porch, either reading or discussing our Fourth of July plans. George pointed across the street at a white pickup truck, wheels and fenders covered with mud. The truck towed a twenty-foot boat. After parking and blocking a driveway, a man in his mid-thirties, left the truck carrying a Miller Lite beer, and stumbled to the front door of the house. As they admitted him, an individual pointed at the boat and spoke, but we couldn't hear what he said.

In ten minutes, a thin college-age parking cop on a bike rode past the boat and stopped in front of the truck. He took out his ticket pad and began writing. The boat owner burst from the front door, carrying a Bud Lite and yelled at the parking cop, "What are you doing?"

"Giving you a ticket. You can't park on the street especially when blocking a driveway."

"He better watch it. He can be arrested for carrying an open alcohol container," George commented.

"It's at least his second beer before 12:30." I said.

"Yes, but they're light beers, so at least he's staying on his diet," Betsy moralized.

"Where am I supposed to park? A fine way to greet tourists on Independence Day!" the boat owner screamed at the cop.

"Sir, I don't know, but you can't park here. And it's illegal to drink beer on a public street."

"I'm on private land. You can't touch me," the boat owner smirked as if he practiced law. He chugged the beer and bent the empty aluminum can in a show of strength to intimidate the young cop.

"Then stay there while I finish writing the ticket."

The boat owner threw the empty can on the ground, jumped in the pickup truck and said "I'm leaving. You won't write me a ticket. I'll be long gone before you finish."

The cop smiled and moved to within six feet of the front of the truck and kept writing as the boat owner gunned the engine.

"Get out of my way, or I'll run you over"

The cop kept writing and didn't respond. The boat owner gunned his engine again and lurched forward, just missing the cop who jumped onto the lawn out the truck's path. He put away his pad, and jumped on his bike and followed the boat weaving down the road.

Simultaneously, without communicating John, George, and I jumped off the porch to follow the action. We heard Betsy yell out, "I bet you chase ambulances too."

John turned his head and screamed, "No we're not lawyers." I guess he forgot I had been practicing law for ten years although I never marketed my practice when I ran.

We caught up to the pickup truck with the boat after it had turned right heading south on Coastal Highway. Red traffic lights stalled the July 4 cars as far as we could see. The cars slowly moved forward when the lights changed to green. The parking cop's bike caught up to the truck, but he didn't approach it. He called on his walky-talky and waited. Fortunately for him real police with guns drawn came running toward the pickup truck from the Dewey Beach police station located only two blocks away. We saw the loud-mouthed boat owner cower in the cab of his truck as the police knocked on his door window and ordered him to get out. The door opened. The boat owner tripped on the floor of the cab and spilled onto the road. Several cops turned him over, handcuffed him, stood him up, demanded his truck keys, and escorted him to the police station. Two cops asked the crowd to disperse while another drove the pickup to the station.

After we returned to the house. Betsy asked, "What happened?"

When we told her, she said, "I should have gone with you."

Armed with our invitations John and I wearing our cleanest t-shirts and shorts drove to Shari's Henlopen address on Rolling Road to attend my first beach party. We had to park a hundred yards from the home, a two story cedar shingled large Cape Cod with four dormers on the front. Low hedges surrounded the back yard where we could see a tent which I assumed held the bar. We followed several individuals walking toward a gap in the hedges which served as the entrance to the party.

We watched as they handed their invitations to the gentleman dressed in pressed white shorts, a formal ruffled shirt and bow tie, covered by a white dinner jacket or the woman in a low-cut black cocktail dress. After looking at each other and our clothes and hesitating for a few seconds, John said, "They must be the hired help, part of the catering service. Let's go, we have invitations."

The crowd milling around the tent must have been caterers since they dressed the same. I gave my ticket to the woman who took it with a forced smile, while John handed his to the man who asked, "I don't know you. Who invited you?"

"Anne Sinclair and Shari Tompkins," I answered.

"Mary, please ask Anne and Shari to come here so they can meet their guests." He left us standing at the entrance, while they admitted others, all more formally dressed. In a few minutes, both women walked to the entrance and greeted us.

"Are these your friends?" the gentleman said.

"Yes," Shari replied. "Can they join us?"

"Of course," the ticket taker said, "I didn't want them to feel lost without you."

As we walked to the tent for our first beer, John said, "I don't believe him. He thought we crashed the party."

"He might have since he's never met you," Shari said.

"I don't think that's the reason. It's our clothes," I said to Shari, as I noticed many of the guests staring at us. Several of the guys had a bemused smile.

"You might be right. Beach casual must have a different meaning in Dewey than in Rehoboth. Have a good time. Don't be self-conscious," Shari said.

"Okay," I said.

"Most of the guys are jealous and would rather be dressed like you. Their girlfriends dictate the dress code. Personally, I'd prefer to wear running or tennis clothes," Anne replied.

With Shari and Anne's help, we enjoyed ourselves. Shari introduced us to her friends. She didn't care about our clothes.

I had no way to judge this party as a beach party it being my first. The backyard surrounded by hedges on three sides and the calm waters of the Rehoboth-Lewes canal provided extensive views of the marsh beyond. I could not stop eating the food on the waiters' trays as they circulated: shrimp, scallops wrapped in bacon, barbecued chicken in peanut sauce, and crab stuffed mushrooms.

Shari and I talked for the entire party. As we left, Shari said, "Anne and I have a court at the Rehoboth Beach public tennis courts for 10:00 a.m. Please join us?"

We agreed without hesitation or consulting each other.

"You are both perfectly dressed for tennis," Anne said.

"John, Shari and Anne could have left us if they weren't so nice. We dressed like bums compared to everyone else. I'm wondering how much of the social life of the beach you know," I said when we drove home.

"Everything about Dewey Beach and its parties, but not much about Henlopen Acres. While I've heard of their parties, I had never been to one. What an experience. Perhaps we should upgrade our wardrobe. So you're embarrassed for a few minutes. Shari couldn't get away from you, and we have a tennis date for tomorrow morning. I say my mission's accomplished."

I didn't respond, not wanting to give him the satisfaction of knowing he had pulled me out of my depression. When we returned to the beach house, both John and I begged off from eating a large traditional beach dinner.

We sipped wine and sat on the porch watching people wobble down the street toward the beach carrying cardboard boxes. John said, "Let's find out what happened to the guy with the boat."

We both walked across the street and I asked a member, "What happened with the boat?"

"The owner spend the night in the Georgetown jail. Most members of our house didn't appreciate his noontime drunken behavior. We're happy he's in jail and not here."

"Steve, make sure you behave tonight. I don't want to be bailing you out," John said, when we returned to our porch.

"Don't worry. I appear to be the sanest person on the block."

"To some women, pursuing two of them in the same house is a capital offense."

I gave him a strange look and didn't respond. At 9:00 p.m. John announced. "It's time to get ready to watch the fireworks."

"I've packed the cooler, Gatorade spiked with vodka.

Two bottles for each of us," Betsy said.

I looked at John and whispered, "Haven't we had enough? We'll get arrested and spend the night with the boater." My voice louder than I had planned attracted smirks and sneers from the others.

"Steve, no one is driving. It's July 4, be patriotic."

Admonished, I joined the group a few minutes later, when they left the porch and mixed with the others moving toward the ocean, hoping Betsy's cooler wouldn't be examined. As we arrived at the beach the light had faded to where everyone looked gray. We let others walk toward the ocean as we sat on a dune at the back of the beach that provided a comprehensive view of the groups huddled together and dispersed along the beach. Betsy handed us our first bottle of Gatorade. Most of the group took a sip, but not wanting to have a hangover for tomorrow's tennis, I placed the bottle in the sand.

After ten minutes a guy joined the group. Everyone said hello except me since I hadn't met him. An unwarranted pang of jealousy shot through my body as he gave and received a passionate kiss from Betsy.

"Carl, this is Steve. It's his first time at the beach," Betsy said, not recognizing my despair.

"Please be nice to him. We're recruiting him to fill Jennifer's spot."

I didn't realize how emotionally the beach would affect me, having gone from zero prospects to two in one day. Now reduced to one. John had more wisdom than I thought in advising me not to expect to have a relationship with Betsy.

"Carl has been a member of the beach house for three years and dated Betsy before he joined," John said. Feeling betrayed I remained silent. He should have told me earlier that Betsy had a boyfriend. If they want me to join their house, I planned to ask for a personal history of its members. A flash of light followed by a loud sound distracted me from my thoughts.

"It's started. Let's drink a toast to Dewey Beach fireworks," Carl said. Everyone except me raised their bottles.

Betsy noticed, "Steve it's not polite to refuse to join in a house toast."

"Betsy, I'm playing tennis tomorrow and don't want to have a hangover."

"What? Did you believe my joke that I spiked the Gatorade with vodka? Everyone's a jock here, either playing tennis, volley ball, or running tomorrow. We don't want hangovers either, and I don't want to go to jail."

Not liking to be the brunt of a joke, I said nothing, but picked up my bottle still not knowing if she told the truth. When I tried to turn the cap, I discovered it hadn't been opened. Unless she had used a hypodermic needle to insert the vodka, I realized Betsy had not lied. My first sip verified her honesty.

The light and sound show continued as I nursed my bruised ego, realizing Betsy had not directed her joke at me but at everyone. As I relaxed I saw a group on the beach scatter in every direction from their original center. "That's the first one," John said pointing to the runners. Simultaneous explosions arose from the vacated center.

"What happened?" I asked.

"They accidently set fire to all the fuses on their fireworks," Carl said.

"Does that happen often?" I said.

"Just wait," John replied.

It happened three other times in the half hour that the beach fireworks lasted, but luckily no one appeared hurt. I wondered if members of the Delaware State Legislature had watched or taken part in the fireworks that night. Perhaps they were part of one of runners dispersing from an explosion. Years later they passed Delaware Code 6901 outlawing personal ownership of fireworks in Delaware.

My anger at John and Betsy dissipated as we returned to the beach house, and I seriously thought of accepting their invitation. I fell asleep looking forward to tomorrow's tennis match.

When I woke up refreshed Sunday morning, I realized my first July 4 day at Dewey Beach had to be the highlight of my beach experiences. Wrong, since I didn't understand the potential entertainment and experience value of joining a beach house.

After a light breakfast of coffee, juice and

croissants, we met Shari and Anne for tennis. Since I only had one woman left to impress, I didn't want to be lethargic on the courts. We played three sets. The first two were mixed doubles with different partners. The women played better than the men. John didn't share my analysis since he readily agreed to play a third set of women versus men. I protested. Shari said, "If you play, when we finish we'll go to our house and make you lunch."

I agreed to trade embarrassment for food. We lost 6-1. The lunch of leftovers from last night's party, exceeded my excitement watching the fireworks. As we left Shari handed me a business card and said, "Call me."

"How much does membership cost?" I asked, as John drove back to the house.

"It's prorated on the time left. I'll give you the exact cost when we get back home."

"Why did you agree to play them? They're better than both of us," I asked.

"Yes. You don't understand women, being married for so long. Of course they were better than us. If we refused to play that would be the last we'd have seen of them. They wanted to find out how we'd react to losing. If we pouted, Shari wouldn't have given you her business card."

"Maybe she can give me lessons."

"I'm sure she will."

Steve's First Woman

Steve moved into a rooming house for college students early in June 1968 after high school graduation. Larry and Ruth Mullen, an immigrant Irish Catholic couple, owned the home and had been renting to students for fourteen years. The home in Flushing, Queens, and a half a block north of Queens Boulevard near St. Johns University was perfect for Steve. He enjoyed his summer between graduation and the start of his freshman year in college.

Steve celebrated his graduation by visiting the local bars in Queens near his new residence. On the second Friday in June after caddying, he returned to his new home to find it empty. He showered, divesting himself of 90-degree heat-induced sweat and dust from a full day of caddying. When clean and dressed for the evening, he wandered into the basement kitchen for a new experience–cooking.

FRANK E HOPKINS

After eating he walked to Queens Boulevard and entered Smith's Bar, a smoke-filled local restaurant with a jukebox playing songs from the fifties and new recordings by the Righteous Brothers. Two rows of tables lined the wall opposite the bar with only ten feet separating the bar from the tables. Several couples danced to *You've Lost that Lovin' Feelin'* on the small dance floor.

Steve ordered a draft and sat at an empty table. He didn't see the curvaceous woman with black hair draped over tanned shoulders, in her late twenties, sitting in the shadows at a table next to him. But, she noticed him. His strong wide shoulders and flat stomach, his black hair framing his light skin, bright innocent blue eyes, and his youth attracted her.

While Steve sipped his beer, he looked at the dancers, fantasizing about meeting several of the girls when he heard, "Excuse me, can I get by?"

Steve looked over his shoulder to see large blue eyes smiling at him, waiting for him to move his chair. Overwhelmed by the cleavage from her loose white blouse less than a foot from his eyes, he said, "Sure," as he stood up and moved his chair.

She gazed at him, locked her eyes with his. "Thanks."

Steve sat down and watched her walk to the women's room in tight cut-off dungaree shorts. He downed the beer and went to the bar and ordered a second. His thoughts ventured away from the girls on the dance floor to the dark-haired blue-eyed woman.

When Steve left the bar, he saw she had returned, her eyes fixed on him. He smiled as he sat in his chair.

"Why don't you join me? It's no fun drinking alone," she said. An older woman had never asked Steve to join her for a drink. Flustered, he didn't know what to say, blushed, chugged half his beer, and moved to her table. "Sure."

"Hi, I'm Mary Parker." She raised her Seven and Seven to her lips, sipped the drink and looked straight into his eyes.

"I'm Steve Lynch."

"I noticed you when you walked into the bar. You looked lost. I've never seen you here before. Is this your first time?"

"Yes, I moved into a college rooming house a few blocks away."

"Go to St. Johns?"

"No, I go to Hofstra. My housemates go to St. Johns."

"You'll like Queens Boulevard. It's safe, with plenty of restaurants, a few movies, and lots of young people."

"I'm just exploring it."

"What's your major?"

"History."

"What are you going to do with a history degree?"

"I don't know, I'm not sure what I'll end up doing. I chose history because I love it."

"It's not good to choose a major just for a profession. I majored in education without examining alternatives. Looking back, I should have chosen a more interesting and stimulating subject. I teach third grade."

"Are you happy teaching?"

"It's fine. I love the kids. I have none, but they're a good substitute."

A slow cha-cha, *Come a Little Bit Closer* by Jay and the Americans, began playing. Mary said, "Can you dance?"

"Yes." Steve stood up.

Mary bent over, exposing more cleavage, thrilling him, as she rose from her seat.

Steve finished his beer and followed her to the dance floor, took her in his arms and counted to pick up the beat. He moved his left foot forward and she effortlessly followed him. Steve enjoyed the way she moved when dancing. She kept her shoulders straight while her legs and hips swayed to the slow rhythm. When he released her, she turned around numbing him by the sight of her tanned athletic legs as they merged into the blue cut-offs, covering her rotating rear. He continued dancing realizing he held a fully-formed woman and not a skinny high school girl.

They danced several fast dances, until a slow Platters' song, *(You've Got) The Magic Touch,* started playing. Mary made no move to return to the table, but grabbed his left hand and slipped her right arm around his back and moved close to him, brushing his body with hers, a sensation he never experienced with Joan, his puritanical Catholic girlfriend. Her strong floral perfume overwhelmed him. Mary whispered in his ear, "I like this song. I'm glad I met you."

"Me too."

"You're the same as me, Irish, with blue eyes and black hair."

Though four inches shorter than Steve, she placed her head sensuously between his face and shoulder. They remained silent for the rest of the song. Steve tried not to show his excitement, but failed. When the dance ended they returned to the table.

"I'm going to get another beer. Do you want anything?" Steve said.

"No thanks. I have plenty of beer at my apartment. Why don't we go there and breathe smoke-free air?"

As they walked the short three blocks west of Smith's Bar to Mary's apartment, Steve wondered how the night would end. Steve's body stiffened when Mary placed her right arm between his left arm and body and smiled, saying, "You're strong. Do you work out?"

"No, I get my muscles from caddying. Carrying two golf bags weighing over fifty pounds each makes you strong. Mary you have a great body," Steve said.

"Thanks, I'm glad you like it. I'm divorced and have to keep my figure to attract men. I run and watch my diet."

"Glad you like muscles."

After reaching the apartment they walked up one flight to her studio. Steve noticed a small kitchen to the left of the door, with a table against the wall next to the refrigerator, one love seat to the right of the door, and a lamp table to the left of the sofa, and a double bed opposite the door. Two doors flanked the bed, one to a closet and the other for the bathroom

"Small isn't it?" Mary said.

"Yes, but it looks practical."

"It's home now. I used to live in a house in Jamaica Estates. I lost it as part of the price for my freedom. Sit on the love seat, and I'll get you a beer."

Steve stared at Mary's body as she reached into the refrigerator to grab two beers.

While she felt anxious, Mary realized Steve felt more nervous. She had never picked up a man, or had sex since she split with her husband. Mary had expressed her sexual frustration to several girlfriends at a women-only dinner. Several of them, divorced for over a year, advised her how to meet willing young men. Though nervous at the prospect, she listened to the description of the techniques they used to relieve their sexual frustration.

Mary walked to the love seat, bent over and handed Steve a beer. She sat next to Steve brushing her leg against his. She felt him shiver when she touched his arm with her fingertips.

"Steve, I hope I'm not tickling you."

"No, that feels good."

"Just relax and enjoy it."

"OK."

Mary took his beer, placed their beers on the lamp table, moved her hands to his face, and pulled him close to her into a long slow, deep, passionate kiss.

Steve's mind raced with the realization he might at last lose his virginity. When she kissed him with warm lips and a tongue exploring his, he didn't know how to react. Never having been kissed that way, he became erect, confused about what she expected him to do. He fondled her breasts.

Mary sensed Steve's excitement and confusion. When she kissed him, she felt the hunger in his response and the shyness of his hand on her breasts. She turned her body, placing one leg between Steve's, feeling his arousal. She reduced the pressure of her leg not wanting Steve to ejaculate. Mary thought Steve behaved like a virgin.

"Steve, that feels good. Let me help you."

He sensed his excitement increasing, and knew his dream might be fulfilled. She became more assertive as she took off her blouse and unhooked her bra.

"Do you like my breasts?

"Your breasts are beautiful."

"Shush," she put her hand around the back of Steve's head, and guided his mouth to her right breast. His excitement increased as he kissed and bit into her nipple.

Mary winced at his roughness and said, "Steve baby slow down, be gentle. We have all night."

"Sorry."

"Are you nervous?"

"Yes."

Mary convinced he had never been with a woman before, decided to make his first experience memorable.

Steve felt inadequate. His body thrilled at her kiss and her leg rubbing against his erection, feared he would mess his pants. His initial panic disappeared when Mary reduced the pressure and movement. He welcomed Mary's offer of her breast, but her reaction to his behavior mortified him. Her calming voice relaxed him.

Mary removed his pants, climbed on top of him, inserted him, and bent over him, her face less than a foot from his, and whispered, "Don't move, I want to feel you inside of me. Do you like it?"

"Yes, it's great. You're so beautiful." The sight of her on top of him with gravity expanding the size of her breasts thrilled him.

"Relax. I'll take care of everything."

Steve, astounded by her body and actions, said nothing.

Mary slowly moved her hips looking at Steve's eyes. Steve responded by looking into her eyes as pleasurable sensations started in his genitals. He moaned.

Mary responded by moving her hips faster until he lost his virginity. The sensation of his first orgasm in a woman overwhelmed Steve, who closed his eyes as the waves of pleasure engulfed him.

Mary held Steve as he went limp. After a minute she asked, "Did you like that?"

"Yes."

"Is this your first time?"

"Yes. Was it that obvious?"

"Don't worry. We're just beginning. If you want I'll teach you how to please a woman this weekend. You're very relaxed now. Just close your eyes and rest."

Seven hours later she woke Steve up. "Baby,

you're a good sleeper. You don't snore or toss and turn."

"What time is it?" Steve said half asleep.

"Why, it's six o'clock, do you have to go somewhere?"

"No," Steve said.

"Good, it's time for another lesson," Mary said anticipating his surprise and her pleasure. "But let's take a shower first." Mary took his hand walked him into the bathroom and turned on the water. Mary took the lead rubbing soap on his front and back. She rinsed him and washed herself.

As they dried each other Steve could not help wondering why he had waited so long to enjoy a real woman. Looking at her body he became excited without her touching him. Steve didn't think of Joan.

After he returned to the bed, Mary started tenderly kissing his mouth, moved his hands to her breasts and fondled his penis. She instructed him on how to caress and gently suck her breasts. She moved away from him and stimulated him orally until he climaxed.

Steve had heard of oral sex and now he had experienced it. Having enjoyed the pleasures of her tongue, lips, and fingers, he wanted to return the favor. "Mary, show me how to do that to you."

Mary lay on her back and told him. After several orgasms, she pulled his body up and inserted him into her. She told him to move slowly and not to prematurely ejaculate, to prolong and intensify their pleasure. When they finished, Mary thought I've waited too long. I'll make Steve addicted to me so we're both satisfied and never frustrated.

"Mary, how do you feel?"

"Good. While I'm happy to be divorced, I miss the steady sex. Steve, you're good looking, strong and young, just what I need for fun. I'm not looking for another husband. I'm too old to be your girlfriend, but I'll be perfect as your lover. If you're a good student we can do this whenever you want."

"I'll try."

Mary used her teaching skills to make him achieve several orgasms and to guarantee Steve's loyalty. Steve forgot all about Joan. He stayed through lunch and returned to his new boarding house after waking up from an afternoon nap when Mary said she planned to meet her girlfriends for dinner. As he left, she said, "Stop by at 10:00 tomorrow morning. We'll continue the lessons."

"I will," Steve replied.

Mary conducted a course in sex education he attended three times a week over the summer until college started. Steve supplemented his academic studies with Mary's training sessions.

Steve told Mary about Joan, and she agreed he should continue his relationship with someone his age. Mary said she had begun dating men in their thirties, and they should continue meeting on a non-emotional sexual basis. Steve had no moral problems sleeping with Mary while still dating Joan.

On a Wednesday evening in the third week of October, Steve and Mary met at Smith's Bar. They had hamburgers for dinner, drank a few beers, and danced several times. After one slow dance to *Yesterday* by the Beatles, Mary said. "Let's go."

That evening they made the most passionate love Steve had ever experienced. Mary surprised him, since their sexual relationship had become predictable and relegated to relieving sexual frustration.

"Steve, we have to talk," Mary said.

"About what?"

"Us. I'm becoming serious with someone."

"That's OK. Just like you don't mind me seeing Joan."

"He wants to spend more time with me and meet my friends which I can't do, if I see you every Friday and several days a week."

"That surprises me, considering the way you made love tonight."

"I wanted to give us something to remember."

"You did. But I'll miss you."

"Don't worry. You're handsome and now that I've trained you to be a great lover, you'll find a substitute soon."

The Romance Life Cycle: Theory F and Your Heart

First Appointment

Paul said, "I used to run marathons. Six months ago I couldn't walk up the stairs without panting. I decided to end the relationship with my girlfriend Susan when on a spring day while working in my garden I noticed I had a hard time breathing and if I continued in my sedentary lifestyle, I might die.

"What does that have to do with breaking up with Susan?" Dr. Eva Mueller, an experienced marriage counselor in her early fifties, asked. She sat in the small office in a chair across from Paul. He tensed up. He sat with the window behind him. Providing her a view of the multi-storied buildings on Wisconsin Avenue in Chevy Chase. Paul noticed she wore a large diamond ring and wedding band. He thought it's good to have a relationship therapist whose marriage worked.

We had been together three years. Her body turned from an athletic wonder into an obese woman. Susan regularly drank wine, ate fatty foods, and was happy when I joined her after she cooked a high caloric meal.. My body looked worse than hers after gaining forty pounds. I could see a real heart attack coming unless I ended the relationship and took care of myself."

Paul Hoffman wore blue slacks and a gray short-sleeve shirt. Dr. Mueller, more relaxed, dressed in a formal business suit.

"So she caused it?" Dr. Mueller asked.

"Yes, I thought so then."

"How do you feel now?"

"I might have been enabling her."

"When did you think that?"

"During my recovery from the breakup."

"Have you recovered?"

"Yes, I've been dieting and running again and in the last six months I've lost the weight I gained."

"If you've recovered, why are you seeing me?"

"I want to understand what happened so I can prevent it from reoccurring in my next relationship."

"Are you sure you're recovered? Your anxiety shows you haven't."

"Perhaps, I'm mostly recovered," Paul said.

"Your relationship could follow a common

scenario, but I'll need more information before I can make a definitive analysis."

"I'll answer your questions. This has happened several times, and I'm wondering if I have a block against developing a long-term commitment."

"How many times?"

"At least five. Six, if you include my ex-wife. But I don't count her since we met in college and married at twenty-two before the age of sexual rationality." Paul wondered if Dr. Mueller thought this too few or too many.

"Paul, I'd count your ex-wife. That's quite a number for someone only thirty-eight. There are many reasons individuals are unsuccessful in forming long-term commitments. Success depends upon finding someone who satisfies your needs and who you satisfy. Some men may want athletic, independent women while others may want Barbie types or something different than their current partner. An unsuitable woman for you could be perfect for someone else. How old is Susan?"

"Thirty-three. Five years younger than me."

"Were the others near your age or in their early twenties?" Dr. Mueller asked.

"Four, a few years younger, and one two years older. I want someone who has shared my history and not someone fifteen years younger."

"Paul, we'll review your past romances to discover your needs and your ability to satisfy a compatible woman's emotional, psychological and physical desires. We'll try to find out why you failed so you don't repeat the same mistakes. Ready to begin?"

"Yes. How should I start?" Paul asked

"Well, we've already learned you prefer women your own age. Please describe the six women physically and summarize other reasons why you dated them."

Paul answered and only stopped talking to listen to clarifying questions.

"Paul, you've filled your life with very attractive, athletic and intelligent women with whom you couldn't develop one successful long-term relationship. How important is the physical condition of your potential mate? Would it be possible to develop an emotional relationship with a non-Barbie girl?" Dr. Muller asked after Paul had finished talking.

"I'm not looking for physical attractiveness as my main criteria. However, I realize if my partner doesn't stay in shape, it will affect my ability to stay thin. Both my parents smoked and were twenty pounds overweight. They died in their fifties during my twenties. They never exercised. My mother died from lung cancer because of smoking, and my father died from a ruptured aneurism from not taking his blood pressure medicine. I vowed to take care of myself and live to my eighties and knew my mate had to have the same goals or else we'd both fail, ruin our health, and die early. I want to develop a deep emotional relationship with a woman who can carry our children and live to old age with me. No Barbie trophy wife for me."

"Good. There might be hope for you. We have no more time today. For next week, examine the beginning of your relationship with Susan, and see if you can find common elements among the five others. We'll discuss what you discovered."

Paul left the first early morning session with Dr. Mueller refreshed and relieved that after five months of debating with himself, he had agreed to seek professional help. He boarded the sixth floor elevator and descended to the public parking garage three levels below the ground floor. He took the rest of the day off and decided to continue his physical recovery by seeing how far he could run on the C&O Canal on that warm May afternoon. The drive through beautiful Chevy Chase and Bethesda to the canal eliminated any remaining depression he felt from losing Susan.

Paul parked at Lock 7 near Glen Echo at noon and trotted west toward Great Falls. After a half-mile warm-up he increased his pace to an eight-minute mile and planned to run until he had to quit from exhaustion.

As he approached Lock 14, he saw what appeared to be a beautiful slim blond, several hundred yards away running toward him. He unconsciously smiled, appreciating her athletic movements and realized his libido, dead since the breakup with Susan, had returned. Paul tried not to stare as they closed the gap by looking at the canal, the surrounding trees, and the tow path. When they were less than fifty yards apart, the blond stopped running. He continued to avoid staring at her until he heard her say, "Paul. Did you lose your job?"

He looked up, "Susan! No, I took the day off. What are you doing here?"

"I run at lunch or in the morning every day to regain my girlish figure. You look different. You must have lost fifty pounds."

"Thanks, you've also lost weight."

Paul's surprise turned defensive, as he remembered hatred in their heated discussions during their breakup. Susan's voice still had a condescending tone. She always overestimated his faults. He knew he couldn't have lost forty pounds since he had not gained that much and wondered if he should have corrected her. He did not.

"Nice seeing you again I have to finish my run before it gets too late," he said as he trotted west toward Great Falls.

Second Appointment

Paul arrived ten minutes early for his second appointment, in contrast to arriving only one minute before his first. A matronly receptionist took his name and directed him, "Please sit down. We'll call you in a few minutes." He noticed the office painted in subdued beige had three interior doors, but advertised five therapists, implying they shared the offices.

Paul wondered if he should tell Dr. Mueller he had met Susan. He decided not to since it had no bearing on his long-term problem.

"Paul, did you have a good week? Are you prepared to discuss the beginnings of your relationship with Susan and contrast it with your other significant girlfriends?"

"Yes."

"How did you meet Susan?"

"We met on-line though the Internet website Match.com. Susan and I appeared to be perfect for each other. We liked the outdoors, ran on the C&O Canal, listened to classical music, and enjoyed the theater. She had a beautiful face and body and the sexiest blond hair."

"Have you met your other significant girlfriends through the Internet?"

"I've met three. I met two others, including my ex-wife, at parties hosted by my friends and the last, before Susan, on a sailing cruise on the Chesapeake Bay."

"So you don't go trolling in bars, but evaluate your long-term potential girlfriends via a third-party intermediary."

"I never thought about it, but you're correct. Is that good or bad?"

"It's good if you want to avoid STDs and early disappointment when you find out she's not the one after a few dates. Your procedure of prescreening potential lovers while it may take longer is more efficient in developing long-term relationships. So you created a favorable impression of Susan by communicating through Match.com. Please discuss your first real meeting."

We had dinner at the Café Deluxe in Cleveland Park, DC over three and a half years ago."

"Did the dinner go well?"

"Extremely."

"What did you talk about?"

"Our background, what we had in common, expanding upon the information in our Match.com profiles."

"Please provide me specific details."

Paul spent fifteen minutes discussing their conversation.

After he finished, Dr. Mueller asked, "Did anything at the dinner bother you then?"

"Yes, she liked dessert, which I never ate. We split a chocolate-brownie-hot-fudge Sundae. She said running controls her weight."

"Both of you agreed to meet again?"

"Yes, we made a date to go running together."

"Did you pay for the dinner?"

"No, we split the check."

"Was this a onetime event, or did she continue to insist on splitting the check?"

"Yes, Susan continued to split our dating expenses. I liked our financial arrangement."

"Did the women in your other five relationships share expenses?"

"Three of them, but not the other two."

"How did this affect your relationship with them?"

"At first everyone attracted me, but as time passed I felt exploited by those who didn't financially contribute to the relationship since I knew both had good incomes."

"Financial equity appears to be an important consideration for you. Since Susan satisfied your financial constraints, can I assume finances did not cause your breakup?"

"Yes."

"Well we've discovered a behavioral trait that must be present to ensure your next relationship lasts. Your partner must earn a decent salary and share expenses."

"Correct. Is that bad?"

"No, it depends on your needs. Did your ex-wife share expenses while you dated?"

"No, my ex-wife's finances don't count since as students neither of us had money."

"Were you financially cheated during the divorce?"

"Yes, I lost our house and had to pay alimony until she remarried three years later."

"Searching for an economically self-sufficient woman is a rational reaction to your divorce. If you had money it might not be as important."

"I agree. I won't date women, no matter how attractive, who don't share expenses."

"That's it for today. For next week please examine the early development of your relationship with Susan and the others to see if you can find common elements, besides finance and athletics. We'll discuss your findings."

After the session, Paul went running on the C&O Canal at lunch time. He avoided Susan by starting his run at Lock 1 in Georgetown. During his run, he worked on his homework assignment. He smiled as he reminisced about running with Susan, going out to dinner and shows, cooking for each other, and the anticipation and joy of making love.

Third Appointment

Paul entered Dr. Mueller's office ready to answer any of her questions for the next fifty minutes.

"Paul, please describe the first six months of your relationship with Susan."

"We spent most of our time together after a month. Susan and I ran together as often as we could on weekends or after work. We liked to go to the Smithsonian or other museums at least once during the weekend. One night a week we'd go to a play, a classical concert, or a movie, and ate at a restaurant twice a week. Both of us liked to cook together instead of going out. This continued for the first six months of our relationship."

"What activities brought the greatest happiness?" Paul discussed them for the next twenty minutes.

"Did you have this the same pattern with your other five relationships?" Dr. Mueller asked when Paul had finished.

"Pretty much. If I felt no mutual attraction, the relationship wouldn't last long. Isn't that normal?"

"Perhaps. However, there's a danger in committing too early; you rarely get to know the person you are committing to within thirty days. The other extreme is the commitment phobic who won't commit after several years together. I advise you to go slower next time and get to know each other."

"Thanks. I'll do that."

"I know you had an Irish Catholic upbringing. Since you didn't mention sex, can I assume you both abstained during your first six months?"

"No! We made love in the first week and continued throughout the first six months."

"Did that occur in your other five relationships?"

"Yes. Why spend time together if you don't satisfy each other sexually?"

"If you don't have a high sex drive, it won't matter to you. But apparently you do. What does this tell you about developing search criteria for your next relationship?"

"I won't spend time with women who aren't interested in sex," Paul said.

"Time's up for today. For next week, please examine the rest of your relationship with Susan to see if you can find additional common elements besides finances, athletics and a strong sex drive. We'll discuss what you discovered."

Paul ran in the evening at six since he didn't want to take a chance on meeting Susan at lunchtime. He drove to his favorite site at Lock 7 on the C&O Canal. After running three miles, he noticed a beautiful, slim, blond several hundred yards away running toward him. He thought it can't be Susan again. When they closed, he said, "Hi Susan, I thought you ran during your lunch hour."

"I used to but after our brief encounter and sparse conversation I hoped I wouldn't see you again if I ran at night."

"Strange I usually run at night. But I guess you couldn't have known that. I figured you didn't want to talk after our breakup," Paul said.

"Paul, we went together for three years and split over six months ago. Let let's be civil to each other."

"I've said nothing argumentative, especially after your comment about my weight."

"I thought I complimented you," Susan replied.

"Your compliments always had a negative meaning which I didn't appreciate."

"You're too sensitive, never hearing the positive in my compliments, only the negative. No wonder we didn't last," Susan said.

Fourth Appointment

Paul entered Dr. Mueller's office wondering if he should mention his two painful encounters with Susan.

"Let's review our earlier meetings, and the search criteria we've developed to help you achieve a long-term relationship," Dr. Mueller said.

"Okay."

"First, your future mate should be near your age. Second, she must be athletic and, third, financially secure. Don't waste your time on young, inactive women who don't share expenses. You should have an easy time screening women with these three criteria. Fourth, don't commit too early. Go beyond your first impressions on Match.com or your friends' descriptions and beyond the first several dates in your evaluation of your potential mates. It takes months to know someone. Fifth, sexual intimacy is important to you. There are many women who married a sexually inept spouse, and have no other experience, but are willing to learn to increase their sexual knowledge. Be patient, but persistent in evaluating a woman's sex drive. If you decide she has less than you need, break off the relationship gently, but end it, or you both will be unhappy."

"I agree. Anything else?"

"We'll see. Were you and Susan faithful to each other?"

"I never cheated and she said she didn't either so I guess we were for three years until we split."

"How about the other relationships?"

"I found two had other lovers."

"How did you react?"

"They both said they'd drop their other lover, but I soon lost interest in them. We argued and broke up within two months."

"So that's a sixth criteria, make sure they're faithful. It may take a while to learn whether they're monogamous. You can ask during the initial period of dating. Some women tell the truth and say they date one man or multiple men while others lie. It may be useful to use the BeenVerified.com or similar apps to see if they have an arrest and conviction record or have had other problems. Paul, you might want to hire a private detective to answer whether she's faithful without letting her know your suspicions."

"Isn't a private detective rather extreme?"

"Do you want to wait until after you're married and go through an expensive divorce?"

"No."

"Then I recommend a private detective if you're thinking of a committed relationship that could lead to marriage."

"I'll consider it."

"Let's switch to another topic. At our first appointment you told me becoming fat caused you to end your relationship with Susan. How did you gain weight?"

"Very slowly. I didn't realize it for the first year. We liked to go to good seafood and Italian restaurants, and we enjoyed cooking meals together."

"Seafood should not have been a problem."

"If we stuck to seafood, but we always had a baked potato and shared a dessert. Since we split the check, we went out at least twice a week. Italian restaurants were a big problem. I liked pizza and pasta with high caloric sauces: Alfredo and pesto."

"What did you cook together?"

"We had bacon and eggs for breakfast, a salad with meat or tuna fish for lunch, and seafood, steak, or pasta, plus vegetables, including potatoes or rice for dinner."

"Did you drink wine with dinner?"

"Yes, we always split a bottle. We liked visiting the local Maryland and Virginia wineries and searching for good wine."

"It's a wonder you didn't gain weight faster."

"We still ran together. I didn't notice I had gained any weight until my pants got tight six months after we started dating. After a year, I had to buy pants with a larger waist size which upset me. Susan told me waists get larger as we grow older. By then I'd gained fifteen pounds. She had gained ten. Our youthful trim bodies had swollen."

"What happened to the frequency of your sexual relations?"

"They declined. We discussed it and agreed that while we still loved each other, it became natural that since we dated for so long we weren't as sexually fascinated with each other as when we first met."

"Did you ever resent her for not wanting sex when you did?"

"Not at first, but by a year and a half, I resented her and we occasionally argued."

"Did she share your resentment?"

"Yes, I believe she did."

"What happened to your joint running during this period?"

"As we gained weight, running became more difficult. Our weight gain accelerated. By the end of our second year, we had stopped running together and rarely ran at all."

"Did you ever wonder if the gain in Susan's weight caused the decline in your sex drive?"

"Not until the beginning of our third year when she had gained twenty pounds. I looked at pictures of her when we first started dating and noticed the overweight woman she had become."

"Do you think she resented you getting fat?"

"Yes, she told me frequently, saying I had changed from the man she fell in love with and she had no desire to have sex with me."

"How did you respond?"

"Viciously, telling her to look in the mirror. I told her to use a wide mirror so she could see her whole body."

"Wow! Did she respond in kind?"

"Yes, she mentioned other faults of mine during our arguments."

"Did you stop or escalate the arguments?"

"Most of the time I escalated them. Occasionally we both realized the arguments were destroying us, and we'd stop, make up and return to our loving relationship."

"How long did the détente last?"

"A month and then we would make snide

remarks and within a week we had full-blown hurtful arguments."

"Did you decide to break up during one of those conflicts?"

"Yes. I didn't tell you how badly my weight gain had affected my health. A pinched nerve in my lower back affected my ability to walk. My doctor told me the extra weight caused it. Susan, in her nastiest moments, called me a prematurely old cripple."

"That's quite a story. Unfortunately, it's too common among my clients. I've documented this behavior and published a professional paper, *A Romance Life Cycle: Theory F and Your Heart*, to help my therapist colleagues diagnose and correct this problem before it's too late to save their clients' relationships. The F in Theory F stands for **Fat**. Gaining weight, a natural part of a romance may ruin the relationship," Dr. Mueller said as she handed Paul a copy of the eight-page document. "Please read it before you date again."

"Are you saying overeating ended our relationship?"

"Yes, there are both physiological and psychological reasons why you couldn't avoid your fate without knowing Theory F."

"What are they so I don't fail next time?"

"Physiologically most men and women don't know how to control their sex drive. Religions try to suppress it, but since the sexual revolution in the 1960s and 1970s most individuals react and do not manage their sex drives. Many species including birds and chimpanzees use food as a bribe for sex. Humans are no different that's why going out to dinner is such a popular date for couples starting a relationship."

"I always wondered why most first dates are dinner," Paul said.

"Cooking together reinforces a couple's pleasure in their relationship. The foods cooked tend to be highly caloric because they taste better than healthy food causing couples to gain weight as their relationship progresses. They reward their cooking with sex which further stimulates them to cook and eat together. The longer this continues, the fatter each becomes causing the frequency of their sexual relations to diminish. The weight gain decreases their sex drive, or their partner becomes unattractive to them."

"Why don't the lovers recognize their self-destructive behavior before it's too late?"

"They're not acting rationally. They develop repetitive behavioral patterns that make them happy which after six months become unbreakable habits they never question and are as addictive as heroin or tobacco."

"You're kidding."

"No, I'm not. Their relationship declines further. Physiologically they need sex, but are repulsed by each other so they argue: not about sex or food, but about any imagined fault they find in their partner. Subconsciously they're trying to drive their partner away and force them to end the relationship. Eventually, they miss having sex and give into their sex drive and make love. After a few times they're satisfied and the fighting resumes. This cycle continues until the fighting becomes so intense, it may go from verbal to physical abuse. One or both partners leave and end the relationship. The psychological impact of the fighting prevents them from successfully reconciling. They will always repeat their destructive behavior after they resume their relationship, and split."

"That explains why marriage counseling often fails."

"Correct. To be successful the intervention on breaking the Theory F cycle has to be made before the serious arguing starts."

"What stage are Susan and I in our relationship?"

"I am afraid you're past the point of no return. Why, have you considered reconciling?"

"Not really. I met her twice running on the C&O Canal by accident. She looked as beautiful as when we first met. However, we had words, which seemed like a continuation of our last conversation."

"Good. I recommend you don't see her again romantically. You'll just be repeating what occurred earlier. You have a strong sex drive, and probably ignore my advice." Dr. Mueller handed Paul a second copy of her Theory F paper. "Make sure she reads and understands that showing love through food preparation can kill it. If you don't follow the advice in the paper, it may take you a year or two to realize your mistake the second time around when you reach the fighting stage and split again."

"I don't want that to happen."

"I had one client before I finished formulating Theory F who tried the same woman four times over eighteen years. He wasted ten of the eighteen years being unhappy with her. His third reconciliation helped me finish Theory F."

"Poor guy."

"I hope I've helped you. This should be your last appointment unless you forget the advice in Theory F."

Paul read Dr. Mueller's paper sitting in his car after leaving her office. It gave him new hope for recapturing the love he and Susan had for each other. He decided to meet her when she finished running, give her the paper and suggest they have dinner to discuss it.

The next day at lunch Paul drove to the C&O Canal to visit their favorite run starting locations. He first stopped in Lock 7 on the Clara Barton Parkway and drove around the parking lot twice looking for her red RAV 4 Toyota. He couldn't find it. Disappointed, but still full of hope, he drove to the Carderock, Old Angler's Inn, and Great Falls entrances with the same result, not locating her car. Paul drove back to work nervously imagining the worst. She had a new boyfriend and didn't run at lunch. The idea that she might have looked for other men surprised him since he hadn't looked for another woman because he had not recovered from her. Paul assumed she felt and behaved the same way. Realizing he could have lost her, devastated him causing a few tears to trickle down his cheeks.

Paul recovered his composure on the drive to work and thought perhaps she only took one day off from running at lunch or had run at night. After work, he repeated his search pattern. No red RAV 4 at Lock 7, the Carderock entrance, or Old Angler's Inn. As he drove to Great Falls, he felt the same loss he had first experienced during the lunch hour.

Ecstasy returned as he viewed the red top of her vehicle. Paul checked the license plate to verify he had the right car. Satisfied, he parked in the closest spot, three cars from hers in another parking lane where he had a clear view. He waited twenty minutes for her to return wondering if she would be alone or with an Adonis, and if she did have a running companion how he would behave.

Susan appeared, wearing powder blue running shorts and a t-shirt, with her blond hair tied in a ponytail. Her beauty overwhelmed him. He gazed around her. She didn't have a running partner. His panic turned to calm. As she walked to her car, Paul left his. She froze when she saw him. "What are you doing here?" she asked.

"I came to see you."

"Why?"

"To apologize for my behavior. Susan, you've been on my mind since we split," Paul paused noticing a quizzical expression on her face.

"Don't stop talking now," Susan said.

"I hurt so much I went to a therapist, to find out what we did wrong, and why I couldn't keep a long-term relationship working with the perfect woman."

"Is this Paul talking? The man who yelled at me and called me obese?"

"Yes, I was also overweight, but didn't realize it."

"That's true. Your therapist must be good." Susan said, smiling.

"She is. I understand our behavior and breakup. A romantic syndrome that dooms many couples caused it."

"Well, that sounds good at least I'm not to blame anymore."

"Neither of us are." He handed her a copy of *A Romance Life Cycle: Theory F and Your Heart*. "My therapist wrote this to explain why many relationships end like ours in arguments and recriminations. Please read it, and I'll call you in a few days, and you can tell me your impression of the paper at dinner in a neutral restaurant. If you don't want to see me again, I understand, but please read it, it might help you in the future."

"Paul you look good, you're not corpulent anymore, but I'm suspicious of your good behavior. I miss the good Paul."

"Susan, you're more beautiful than ever. I miss you too."

"I'll read the document."

Susan called him the next evening. "I read the paper. Very interesting. Why don't you come here for dinner tomorrow night so we can talk about it? I don't want to talk about something so important in a noisy restaurant."

"What time?" Paul said, overwhelmed by her call and words.

"Seven. Just so you don't worry, I'll be serving baked salmon and a garden salad with red wine and balsamic vinegar dressing. We'll be drinking unsweetened ice tea."

Three years later Dr. Mueller, while hiking on the C&O Canal, noticed her former patient Paul Hoffman walking toward her. As he approached within ten feet she said, "Paul, Dr. Mueller, you were my patient years ago."

"I remember. Thanks for all your help."

"What are you pushing?"

"One result of your sessions. My daughter Sarah."

Dr. Mueller looked in the baby carriage and exclaimed, "She's beautiful. How old?"

"Seven months."

"Did you marry the woman we talked about?"

"Yes. She's running ahead of us. You changed our lives. We now have to run alone and in shifts."

Santa Claus Stories

On a Friday evening in June, Pat Raymond drove from upstate New York to O'Neill's Bar in Rockville Centre, New York for a few beers. It always refreshed him when he entered the dimly lit restaurant with its odor of stale beer, black and white tiled floor, polished dark mahogany chairs, tables and booths.

Pat spent many years in O'Neill's, a typical Irish family bar in the New York City area, patronized by working-class families. The bar provided cheap drinks and wholesome Irish food. Pat had not been in Rockville Centre or at O'Neill's for four years. Nothing had changed. He spotted Tom Fitzsimmons at the bar. Pat sat on a stool next to him and ordered a beer. The first sip always surprised him with how good beer tasted after a long drive.

"Pat, what are you doing here?" Tom asked.

"I'm here for Jennifer's wedding."

"Did you bring your family?"

"No. Anne stayed behind in Binghamton with the kids. At one and three they're too young to travel. How do you feel about your old girlfriend, Jennifer, getting married?" Pat asked.

"Jennifer dumped me twelve years ago so I thought I was over her. But it hurt when I heard she became engaged. I drank for two days, realized that wasn't a solution, and sobered up. Two weeks ago she surprised me by sending an invitation."

"Are you going?" Pat asked.

"Originally, I planned to skip the wedding. I guess my ego still hadn't recovered from our last argument. However, since her family lives here, I occasionally see her. We never bring up the past, so I decided to go."

"Good, we should have a great time seeing our friends return to town fourteen years after high school graduation."

"Pat, you know me. Never want to miss a good party."

"Tom, I don't party the way I used to. Haven't seen you in over four years. Still working at New York Met Insurance in the city?"

"No. Left three years ago. They wouldn't promote me since I didn't have a college degree, so I quit."

"Didn't you finish your degree at night school at Hofstra?"

"No, working full time and attending college were too tough for me. I stopped going three years ago."

"Too bad. Where do you work now?"

"I've had several jobs. Now I sell cars at the local Ford dealer," Tom replied.

Pat remembered Tom always made bad choices and rarely finished what he started. The discussion depressed him so he changed the subject. "Is the food still good here?"

"Just like it's always been. Interested in dinner?"

"Yes." The bartender overheard and placed menus in front of them.

"Pat, do you have a successful career?"

"Well, I got tenure at Binghamton University last year. So I now have a job for life if I want it."

"Does Anne like the cold winters?"

"She loves them since we took up skiing a few years ago. She told me it's a perfect location for raising children. I'm sure she'll never let me leave until the children are gone."

"That's great. I've always wanted to talk to you about your success and my failures."

"Are you sure?"

"Yes, I can't figure it out. Both of us went to the same high school and worked during college yet look at the difference."

"Let's not talk at the bar. There's a private booth

where we can be alone and eat dinner." Pat didn't want to embarrass his old friend, or get into a heated argument in front of others if Tom lost his temper. Pat turned to the bartender, "I'll have the Shepherd's Pie and another draft. We're moving to the table in the corner."

"Your glass is half full. I'll bring the next one with the meal," the bartender said. He looked at Tom, "What'll you have?"

"Another beer and a Ruben."

As they sat at the table, Pat asked, "Are you sure you want to do this?"

"Yes, I can't afford to go to a shrink."

"Tom, I'm an economist, not a clinical therapist. But since I've known you for years, I have a few ideas. Before I start, promise no matter how much you get pissed off at what I say you won't get mad, punch me, or end our friendship."

"It must really be bad. I promise to behave."

"Okay. You've accepted too many Santa Claus Stories."

"What does that mean?" Tom said, wondering if Pat planned to deliver a college lecture.

"Tom, I published an academic paper on the topic last year. It caused quite a bit of controversy in my profession, many of whom assume humans are guided by rational behavior in making economic decisions. My view of economic decision-making differs from their simplistic view. Individuals addicted to drugs or alcohol don't make rational decisions to improve their welfare. Their driving force is getting the next fix. Religious zealots behave according to their religious teachings rather than rational behavior, joining a religious war that could lead to their death. Humans behave according to their learned view of the world. Santa Claus Stories explain part of their behavior."

"Pat, that's a little abstract for me. Remember, you have a Ph.D. and I didn't graduate from college. Simplify it and make it specific to me."

"Of course," Pat said, well at least he's not upset at me yet. "Let me define the term Santa Claus Story."

"Please do."

"Santa Claus Stories are constructs used by parents, political, or religious authorities to control behavior. All children are exposed to Santa Claus Stories designed to guide their behavior. Santa Claus Stories are untrue, but they're successful until the individual governed by the Santa Claus Stories receives overwhelming information they're false. The Santa Claus Stories' impact on behavior is implanted on the brain stem that controls our basic actions in a reflex manner rather than through careful conscious decisions.

"The original Santa Claus Story encouraged children to behave. Kids believe Santa Claus knows if they're naughty or nice. If they're naughty, they'll receive lumps of coal for Christmas, but if they're nice, they'll be given presents that will make them happy.

"Religions use their own versions of Santa Claus Stories to control people. If you commit a sin, particularly related to enjoying sex, you'll go to hell and experience eternal damnation. If you don't sin, you'll enjoy bliss in heaven forever," Pat finished.

"Sounds logical, but how does that pertain to me?"

"I'm concerned if I go on, you'll get mad."

"I won't."

"Let's examine your behavior after puberty, in relation to girls, Blacks, going to college, and abortions."

"That's quite a list. Do we have time?"

"Yes."

The bartender delivered their meals and beers giving Pat a chance to pause in his explanation. He watched Tom's hands, which didn't shake, as he used a knife and fork to cut the ample Ruben. Pat reasoned well he's not drunk so maybe I get by tonight without getting into a physical fight. The Shepherd's Pie tasted better than he remembered. The serving size for both meals had increased from ten years ago. Pat glanced around the bar and guessed he had a lower body mass index than anyone else.

"I needed this," Tom said, after several bites,

"Go ahead whenever you're ready."

"Are you still a practicing Catholic?"

"No, I gave it up years ago, when I realized it's impossible to live according to their teachings: including heterosexual prohibitions; political views on society; and the hypocrisy about priests abusing young boys and the hierarchy not doing anything to stop them, but sending them to another parish so they can continue."

"Those are good reasons to renounce your faith but you took too long." Pat paused so he could swallow a forkful of Shepherd's Pie and drink a few ounces of beer.

"Maybe I'm a little slow," Tom replied as he cut and ate a piece of the Ruben.

They both stopped talking and ate for several minutes until their appetites waned.

"Tom, I remember your personality changed when you reach thirteen and discovered girls. You used to be an extrovert before the church preached the impossible Santa Claus Story of not even being allowed to think of girls when your hormones drove you to imagine their bodies in various stages of undress all the time," Pat said.

"I remember vividly. Knew I would go to hell. I thought no one else had the same problem."

"We all did. We played with ourselves to relieve the tension. Eventually, we realized the Church's sexual prohibitions were another Santa Claus Story, although we didn't use those terms. They didn't want teenage girls to get pregnant and so they filled us with fear of eternal damnation if we approached them. We adjusted and by fifteen we pursued girls with abandon."

"That's true. I withdrew and feared teenage girls. I didn't want to go to hell more than I worried about heaven. At four, I knew the reality of and the difference between heaven and hell. I found it hard to conceptualize heaven, but imagined the pain of hell's eternal fire as the same as touching my whole body to a hot iron forever," Tom said.

"See, you continued to accept the sex version of the Santa Claus Stories well after your friends rejected it. My hypothesis stands."

"True, but I outgrew that problem at seventeen when I started dating Jennifer."

"But your acceptance of the Church's Santa Claus Story made you behave that way in high school?" Pat said.

"I hated high school."

"Let's talk about Jennifer later. You didn't always blindly follow Santa Claus Story rules of behavior. Remember when we first went caddying at fourteen and the stories we heard about Blacks before we went to the golf course."

"Pretty bad and untrue." Tom replied.

"As we left the caddy yard that first day, I said, 'I'm starved. Let's go to my house and get something to eat.'"

"Yes. The hot dog they bought us at the snack stand didn't fill me. Remember how we felt that first day?" Tom replied.

"Exhausted, but great. Quite a day. I had never been on a golf course before."

"My shoulder hurt, but we made five bucks! That's more than I make in a month from neighborhood odd jobs. Those golf bags must weigh over thirty pounds, made from leather and stuffed with clubs, balls, sweaters, and umbrellas."

"I told you about a conversation I had with Willie, a black man. Willie's stories reminded me of my grandparent's struggles when they emigrated from Ireland to America to escape English discrimination."

"It's the same old story of entering the American mainstream, except Willie's family came as slaves, while ours left serfdom in Ireland." Tom responded.

"Yeah, it's amazing that the Irish, who the English treated as slaves, are racist. Willie the first Black adult I had ever talked to, treated me with more respect than most of my father's friends. Willie didn't appear like the Blacks my father described."

"It isn't the first Santa Claus Story our parents have told us. The Black guy I caddied with treated me the same way," Tom said.

"So much for false racist black stereotypes perpetuated by the Irish," Pat said.

"The government should outlaw Santa Claus Stories beginning with the first one our parents tell us: to be good or Santa Claus won't bring us presents. It's traumatic when young kids learn Santa Claus lies. It causes them to lose respect for their parents," Tom said.

"You rejected the black inferiority Santa Claus Story because over the summer we saw evidence at the golf course that overwhelmed our parent's stories."

"I'm glad I didn't grow into a bigot," Tom said.

"You made a bad Santa Claus Story decision on college. We both caddied, which along with college loans paid for my education. But you listened to your parents and went a traditional route. You said they told you to get a job with a real company so if you didn't get the degree, you have a long stable career with a good pension. The Santa Claus Story about employment kept millions as vassals to large companies, afraid to leave. Many companies abandoned that story when they chased cheap labor to the South and then overseas. The promise of long-term employment with a pension Santa Claus Story had already ended when you accepted it," Pat said.

"True. My parents convinced me not to accept the risk of caddying and working odd jobs until I got a degree. I didn't want to fail, not finish college, and become an unskilled worker, but guess what; you don't need skills to sell cars, just a smile and a sense of blarney. Look at you, you took the risk, and you're now a tenured college professor."

"I remember right here in O'Neill's, Steve and I tried to convince you that your approach had to fail. I said, 'After a two-hour commute to and from Manhattan and a half hour drive to Hofstra you'd be too tired to study.'

Steve told you, 'It would take you eight years for what we planned to do in four. That you could more than pay for college loans you needed to go full time with four years of extra income.' When you told me, 'I'll make less as a clerk in an office than we did caddying and parking cars, I felt sorry for you.' We thought you hopeless since you wouldn't listen to our arguments."

"True, but why did I behave that way?" Tom said.

"I don't know. But you have to change. Let's go back to Jennifer. Your views on abortion killed your relationship. I still remember and can repeat your arguments with Steve and me eleven years ago in this bar."

Steve, drinking his second beer asked, "Tom, why aren't you pro-choice? You'll meet more willing girls at pro-choice meetings than in church.".

"Don't laugh. My earliest memories convinced me abortion is wrong. I lived and remembered being conscious in the womb. I remember turning, warmth, and darkness; I remember the mystery of my early existence. I turned a slow somersault and warmth enveloped me. I felt movement around me as I rolled in the darkness toward a distant white light. This perception had no beginning and appeared to continue forever. Finally, the light invaded my senses and life outside the womb began," Tom responded, "I oppose abortion since I remember being alive in the womb."

"Don't worry, Steve. That's been his standard response since he was a freshman in high school," Pat said.

"Really! You can't expect us to accept that you remember life in the womb. My glass is empty. I'll buy another round," Steve said.

After the beers arrived, Pat said, "Tom, as I've said for years, it's absurd to have those supposed memories guide your behavior. It's probably a dream you had at two or three. Don't tell me you wouldn't ask Jennifer to have an abortion if you knocked her up."

"There's no chance she'll get pregnant," Tom replied.

"The Church has conditioned you against abortion, and your subconscious has provided a justification," Steve said.

"You guys take life too seriously. The Church is BS. I've learned to relax and enjoy life and not complain about my

childhood. The Church uses a Santa Claus Story to bribe teenagers to abstain from sex with the promise of heaven and fear of hell. Preventing pregnancy, not obtaining heaven, is their real goal. As we grew up, we recognized entering heaven occurs in old age, while teenage girls surrounded us. We learned girls wouldn't become pregnant if we used birth control," Pat said.

"Yeah, now every guy wants to meet a girl who's outgrown the Church," Steve said.

"Jennifer hasn't. She's becoming more religious every day," Tom commented.

"Find another girl. Jennifer could be hung up on chastity for life," Pat said.

Tom stuck with Jennifer and within six months they became lovers and planned to get married in two years when she graduated from C.W. Post. She lost her Catholic faith in her second year of studying liberal arts. After they married, Tom planned to quit his job after she started working so he could go to Hofstra full time. They decided to postpone having children until after Tom graduated. But the plan for a perfect life didn't work out. Jennifer became pregnant in her junior year.

"Pat, I should have listened to you and Steve then. But I acted too stubborn to admit I could have been wrong, when Jennifer asked for my help in getting an abortion. She wanted to hide her pregnancy from her religious family, afraid it would break them apart.

"I remember. Jennifer asked me for financial help, but I opposed the abortion. I repeated my story of life in the womb which she had heard earlier. We argued for several days. Finally she said, 'This isn't going to work out. I want to end our relationship.' She confided in her older brother who helped her. Her parents never found out," Tom said, breathing slowly, still trying to hold back his reaction to ending the relationship.

"The Church's Santa Claus Story that abortion is murder ruined your life. Twenty years earlier the Supreme Court told us women control their bodies, not male religious ministers, but you didn't believe them. You readily accepted the Church's story," Pat said.

"It's true. After Jennifer dumped me, I lost interest in school and work and began to drink. It's surprising I didn't lose my job earlier, even though it only required high school skills. I next saw Jennifer five years after we split, on the Long Island Railroad going to the city. She had spent the weekend with her family. I learned she had graduated from college, moved to Brooklyn, and had a great job at an advertising agency. She accepted my apology, but we both knew too much time had passed to rekindle the relationship. Her life had changed so much and mine hadn't. I saw her several times after that before I received her wedding invitation."

"Tom, I'm glad you're going. You know your life isn't over."

"If I don't change, it is."

"Do you agree with my analysis?"

"Yes. I like the way you defined it in terms of Santa Claus Stories."

"Go back to college and catch up with the rest of us. We have plenty of students in their thirties at Binghamton. They're some of our best. They know they've screwed up once and don't want to do it again," Pat advised.

At seven Steve strolled into O'Neill's, spotted Pat and Tom and walked over to their table. "Hi, I drove up from Washington, hoping you guys would be here."

"Do you enjoy being a lawyer at Justice?" Pat asked.

"Yeah, I love it. What have you both been doing?"

"Talking about old times," Tom replied.

"They were great weren't they?" Steve said.

The Ski Trip

Ten years ago one of our friends and co-workers, Dennis, divorced his wife of sixteen years. He found he couldn't cope with the single life and became depressed within six months of being alone. In January, Dennis asked Ron and me, both divorced, to join him at the Café Deluxe in Tyson's Corner, Virginia on Friday night to tell him how to meet women.

"I'll be there, bring your laptop," I said.

Ron and I were not playboys, just two men in their early forties, who ended their marriages and enjoyed the company of women. They appeared to reciprocate, both of us having all our dark hair, but no middle-aged paunches. Ron thin and tall at over six feet looked thirty-five years old at the most. At three inches shorter, with an athletic body and an outgoing personality, I had no problems meeting women, and I looked my age.

Arriving early, we sat at a small table next to the window looking at the stalled rush hour traffic on International Drive. The waitress took our beer orders, and we declined the food menus.

"Thanks for coming. I want to use your knowledge so I don't have to repeat the mistakes you may have made in meeting women," Dennis said.

"Dennis, you expect us to give you our hard earned techniques, sometimes learned through painful experiences, for free," Ron asked. "So that after we train you, you can steal our women."

"No, I'm paying for this by buying the first three rounds. Anymore and I can't drive."

"Jerry, that's a fair price for our years of wisdom," Ron said.

"Agreed, I'll start. Where did Willy Sutton go?" I asked.

"I didn't know Sutton, the bank robber, was single and went looking for women," Dennis replied.

"Sutton earned his living robbing banks. When asked 'Why do you rob banks', he replied, 'That's where the money is.' Dennis, you have to go where the single women are," I explained.

"Single women live everywhere in Washington, DC. Join a club. I belong to rock climbing, tennis, and ski clubs full of athletic, attractive, professional women," Ron said.

"Ron, I'm not as athletic and outgoing as you.

Skiing is my only sport," Dennis said.

"Perfect! Jerry and I are going skiing next weekend at Sugarbush in Vermont," Ron replied, "Join us."

"I'm not that good a skier."

"Dennis, you're going to meet women, not for the skiing. The trip will also improve your skiing. I'll give you a lesson. I used to be a ski instructor at Snowbird, Utah," Ron replied.

"Take your laptop out of your briefcase. You can sign up now," I said.

"Now?"

"If you're as lonely as you said, yes now. You asked for our advice. If you don't follow it, there's no incentive for us to give anymore."

"Don't forget the beer. This process could take months," Ron said.

Dennis reluctantly put his computer on the table. Ron handed him a business card, *Vermont Ski Trips*, with a phone number and website address. "How much does this cost?" he asked.

"If we can afford it, you can too," Ron said.

Dennis hesitated, but threatened by our stern looks filled out the trip registration.

"The ski trip is a onetime event. Let me show you how to access most of the single women in the Washington, DC area. Type in http://www.pof.com in your browser, and we'll teach you the wonders of sexual social networking."

After explaining the operations of dating sites to Dennis, showing him how to find women to meet his expectations, we drank one more beer, and left. We vowed to have a great time and match Dennis with the woman of his dreams.

We arrived at the bus station at six in the evening for our twelve hour drive to Vermont. I had great expectations on Friday, hoping we could sit next to three available attractive women and show Dennis how easy he can meet women. Unfortunately, the women sat together in the front of the bus and by the time we boarded, the remaining open seats were in the back. Several of the passengers had guitars and played and sang different songs as we pulled out of the city. We asked to be placed on the quiet, rather than the party bus, so we could sleep and be ready to ski when we arrived. Both buses permitted alcohol. The more the skiers drank, the louder the singing became as the guitar players tried to outdo each other. I ate my sandwich and drank my last beer at eight and tried to read.

Dennis who sat next to me on the aisle said, "Are these ski crowds always this rowdy?"

"Yes, they're letting out their pent up frustration from work."

"Some of them are drunk. I hope I never lose control like they have. Is drinking a normal part of single life?"

"For many people but not for Ron and me."

"How are we going to get any sleep?" Dennis asked.

"At ten, the bus driver will ask for quiet."

After our conversation, I leaned against the window, covered myself with a blanket and tried to continue reading. Sleep came in less than a minute.

A loud nasal noise woke me up around eleven. One person in the seat behind and one in the seat in front snored in bellicose terms, the noise rising and falling out of sequence with each other. Gazing at Dennis I noticed he wasn't sleeping. He had a disturbed look on his face. I wondered if he regretted agreeing to ski with us. "Dennis, are you okay?"

"No I can't sleep with this noise."

Reaching into my backpack, I took out two small packages and handed Dennis one. "Put these earplugs in. Not all buses are noisy, but I came prepared."

Ron slept though out our brief conversation. Dennis closed his eyes, and exhaustion overcame him as he relaxed and breathed in a slow quiet melodic rhythm. Well, I thought, if he met a woman, she wouldn't kick him out of her bed because he snored.

The next disturbance occurred toward morning when the bus driver slammed on the brakes. Without seatbelts we flew forward hitting the back of the chair in front of us. I heard a screaming uproar from those woken up from deep sleep, trying to get their bearings. I felt blood collecting on my forehead from a small abrasion. Dennis and Ron escaped injury. Other voices yelled, "I'm bleeding."

After stopping, the bus the driver turned on the lights and asked, "Is anyone injured?"

The only responses concerned bleeding. The driver walked down the aisle with a first-aid kit dispensing bandages to those who needed them.

"I'm sorry for the abrupt stop, but a car cut us off, and I had to apply the brakes, or we would have hit it. The driver must have been drunk. After we stopped, he kept swerving and hit a tree. He's okay. He got out of his car and looked at the crumpled fender and hood bent around the tree," the bus driver said.

One passenger asked, "How long to Sugarbush?"

"Less than an hour."

Ron had no problem going back to sleep, but Dennis told me after we arrived, he stayed awake. I fell asleep after ten minutes, but woke up tired when the bus driver turned on the lights and announced, "We've arrived at Sugarbush." The passengers cheered. The bus ride exhausted two of the three of us.

We left the bus and our trip leader handed us the weekend's ski, breakfast and dinner meal tickets. He gave us instructions on getting our luggage and directed us to the hotel desk. A placard at the desk stated, "Sign in here, and check your luggage. Rooms can be entered after 4:00 p.m. Return to pick up your keys. If you are skiing today, do not check in your skiing equipment." Fortunately, the hotel had three clerks on duty who processed all of us within fifteen minutes.

At 7:30 our exhaustion fled, the smell of breakfast coffee, bacon and eggs, wafting from the buffet tables in the Timbers Restaurant turned us ravenous. Since the ski slopes did not open till 9:00 a.m., we ate a sumptuous breakfast. We loaded the plates as if we were teenage athletes, with scrambled eggs, sausage, bacon, home fries, waffles and fruit. We stuffed ourselves and none of us could finish everything on our plates.

Dennis started our breakfast conversation asking, "Is the bus ride always that bad?" in a tone of voice implying he wasn't happy.

Ron answered, "No, every other bus trip I've had is uneventful. I've been on eighteen."

"I've never had any problems before last night," I said.

We walked to the Lincoln Peak section of Sugarbush and went to the beginner's slopes to warm up. The temperature hovered in the high teens, and the sky clear, with a bright sun illuminating the morning slopes–a perfect ski day.

"Ron, remember you said you'd give me a lesson," Dennis said.

"Get on the lift with Jerry, and I'll meet you there."

At the top of the Easy Rider chair lift Ron said, "Dennis, I'll ski a hundred yards down and stop, and motion you to ski toward me, and I'll look at your form."

When Ron waved his arm, I said, "Go ahead Dennis."

"Why don't you go first?"

"I'm a good skier. If you fall, I don't want to climb up the mountain to help you," I said to Dennis, whose hesitancy and heavy breathing showed his fear. "Go ahead, and don't worry about falling. If you don't fall you're not pushing your limits on the mountain."

Shamed, Dennis pointed his skis toward Ron, pushed off with his poles and headed toward him making perfect turns and skiing under control. I followed twenty yards behind. At the bottom, Ron yelled, "Dennis, you don't need a lesson, you need confidence. You should have no problem skiing with us or any women you meet. I don't want you to complain again. If you're half as good as meeting women as you are skiing, you should go home happy."

I watched Dennis beam as Ron talked. I knew he wasn't that good a skier, but as a seasoned instructor, Ron knew the importance of self-assurance in skiing and meeting women. Dennis and I skied the intermediate slopes on Gadd Peak that morning while Ron skied on the expert slopes on Castlerock Peak.

We met for lunch at the Castlerock Pub. Famished from skiing, Ron ordered the Vermont Bacon Blue Burger, Dennis settled on the Turkey Ruben, while I dined on the exotic Spicy Tuna Tostada. We sat at a table next to the window to watch the skiers. Several of the women on the bus joined us. They talked about their morning and how great a time they had. Since they were in their early twenties, it became obvious they had no romantic interest in us, especially when Mary, a twenty-one year old recent college graduate, asked, "Have you met any women your age?" Dennis looked crestfallen at these words.

Ron said, "I skied with several women this morning. Dennis did you?"

Dennis shook his head no.

Mary said, "Dennis, you probably rode the lift with Jerry. You'll meet no one that way. Go on the single lane and maneuver yourself until you're paired with a woman. That's what we do with men. Unfortunately the ski clothes hide our age. I met men in their fifties hitting on me when I started talking. They may have thought I was over thirty."

"We'll try your approach after lunch," I said, glancing at Dennis whose face showed fear. I felt stupid, a successful single man being told by a twenty-one year old girl how to meet women.

After lunch, Ron and I headed to the expert slopes while Dennis stayed on the intermediate slopes.

"Remember what Mary told you. Get in the singles line and sit next to a woman and talk to her. If she's from our area suggest you ski together. After the run, if you both like each other, keep skiing together. Ask her to dinner. Don't worry about us," I said.

Dennis looked lost as he went to the single line of the Valley House lift. Ron and I did not see him until we met for après-ski drinks at the Timbers Restaurant.

Dennis came in last with a big smile, walked to our table and said, "I'm having fun."

We ordered beers and split two Baskets of Fries.

"Did you meet anyone?" I asked.

"Many. Most came from Boston or New York, I even skied with three. I skied better than two of them. Now, I'm back in the single life. I met one from Philadelphia, but that's too far from Falls Church."

"Dennis, Philadelphia is in range, especially since you'd have to stay over and not drive home," I said. "My wife lived in Albany, New York before we were married, and the commuting helped the relationship."

"How did that work out?" Dennis asked.

"We're divorced."

"So it failed."

"No. Our marriage lasted ten years."

"I want to meet someone to marry and stay together forever. I don't want to get divorced again."

"Good luck. Then don't get married, just live happily in sin. Over seventy percent of second marriages don't last," I replied.

"Dennis, did you meet a woman who lives near us?" Ron asked.

"Yes. A woman from Baltimore. We had a great conversation."

"Did you ski with her?" I asked.

"No, I found out I couldn't keep up with her. S h e told me she was on the U.S. Olympic ski team. I didn't think I'd impress her."

"Good move. Recognize when to cut your losses and move on," I said.

"Dennis, I'm glad you're having a good time," Ron said.

"So far, even including the bus ride, it's the best weekend I've had since the divorce."

Buoyed by Dennis' reaction, we enjoyed dinner at the Timbers. We took a nap and showered before going out dancing and trolling for women at nine.

A shuttle took us to the Slide Brook Tavern, where a DJ played old songs from the seventies and eighties, popular when we attended high school and college. We didn't see Mary or her friends. When we walked in, Dennis looked around and saw middle-aged women who had not lost their figures drinking beer or sipping wine. Dennis asked, "You have to show me how to meet those beautiful women at the bar."

"No problem. It's easy. I have it down to a science. Just don't fear rejection," I said.

"Unfortunately, with women I do," Dennis said.

"Jerry's system will cure you," Ron said, hungrily scanning the restaurant.

"See the women lined up at the bar?" I said. "I'm going to start at the right and ask the first woman to dance and if she says no, I'll ask the next one on her left and if she declines, I'll keep asking them to dance until at least one of them accepts."

"What if no one wants to dance?"

"Never happen. They're single and their standing at the bar. The women in relationships sit at tables with their partners."

Dennis looked around the room, "You're right."

The first woman, I asked smiled and said, "Lead

the way."

We danced to two songs: *Billie Jean* and *Celebration*, talking whenever the music wasn't too loud. She introduced herself as Alice and told me she taught high school in Baltimore. She wore her black hair in a ponytail, had a slim figure, hidden by a blue ski sweater, and stood a few inches shorter than me. A perfect woman. Her gyrations showed she had more energy than I did. At the end of the second dance, I didn't admit fatigue, but I guess she heard my heavy breathing and said, "Let's sit the next one out and talk."

"Lead the way," I replied.

Alice laughed as we left the dance floor. Standing a few feet from the bar, Dennis, and Ron, she asked, "Can I get you a beer?"

Ron, who had been talking to Dennis, told me the next morning, "When she offered to buy the first round, Dennis couldn't believe it and mumbled 'Christ' under his breath."

After Alice handed me a Heineken, I introduced her to Dennis and Ron. She introduced us to three of her teaching friends: Nancy, Theresa and Peggy. The seven of us drank and danced, exchanging partners until eleven, when Alice said, "Let's go to our townhouse for dessert." The women cracked up, while Ron and I smiled, but Dennis looked perplexed. "We have ice cream," she added, to clarify any miscommunication.

"I love ice cream," Dennis said, which caused the four women, Ron and me to laugh. Dennis looked like he could not understand why we were laughing and said, "We don't have a car. We took the shuttle here."

"We can drive you in our van," Alice said.

The townhouse, located less than three hundred yards from our condo, had three floors, with a bedroom in the basement, living room and kitchen on the first floor and two bedrooms on the second floor. The furniture had a New England country look. We first entered and stood in the living room wondering about the seating arrangements, when Alice asked, "Who wants ice cream?" The other three women declined. The three men accepted.

"Sit down. I'll bring it. Jerry take the love seat, I'll join you later."

Ron and Nancy sat close together in two chairs separated by a lamp table, while Jerry, Theresa and Peggy, reclined on the sofa. Peggy insisted Dennis sit between them. Ron beamed as he whispered to Nancy, a tall blue-eyed blond, who after taking off her sweater revealed a perfect Nordic body, slim with appropriately placed curves.

Dennis smiled like a child being given a large box of chocolates, sitting between the two women.

Theresa, a dark-skinned Italian, about Dennis's

height, showed her voluptuous figure. Peggy, a red-haired thin Irish women a few inches shorter than Dennis, caressed his hair as she talked.

Alice brought four dishes of vanilla and chocolate into the living room on a bright wooden oak tray. She gave herself the smallest serving. After we finished the ice cream, Nancy took the empty dishes back to the kitchen and announced, "I'm going to give Ron a tour of the townhouse." They went upstairs, but never came back down.

Alice and I started kissing and fondling each other. Occasionally, I opened my eyes and saw Theresa and Peggy rubbing Dennis' back and arms and each exchanging kisses with him. Lucky man, he scores twice on his first try. "Let's go upstairs," Alice whispered.

Alice's alarm woke me up at 7:30. She brushed my hair with her hands and said, "Time to get up. We want to make the first chairlift. There's a spare toothbrush in the bathroom."

"Thanks. I enjoyed last night," I said groggily. When I returned, she kissed me platonically and handed me a piece of paper with her address and phone number, saying, "Call me." I handed her my business card.

Alice put her finger to her lips and whispered, "Quiet, the others may still be asleep," as she led me downstairs. Ron and Nancy sipped coffee in the kitchen, but the others had not left the basement.

Ron stood up and said, "We'll see you on the slopes."

We went outside, "I'm famished. Let's go to Timbers for breakfast," Ron said.

"I'll join you. What do you think of Dennis' luck?"

"Dennis will want to move here."

The restaurant teemed with noisy skiers eager for the first chair lift to start. We spotted Mary and a few of her friends and joined them after we filled our breakfast tray with less food than yesterday's breakfast.

Mary greeted us, "Hi guys, I hear you had a great time last night."

"Who told you that?"

"Dennis." We left the condo building at the same time.

"Dennis!" we both exclaimed.

"Yes, he said on his way to church."

"Church!"

"Are you both deaf, asking me to repeat my words to make sure you heard me," Mary said.

"No," I replied, "We thought he hadn't left the townhouse."

Rather than wait for Dennis, Ron and I went skiing on the expert slopes and had lunch at the

Castlerock Pub with the women we met last night. They left Sugarbush for the long drive home after eating, but not before Ron and I had made arrangements to see them again.

Later in the afternoon, Dennis reappeared at the top of the Castlerock Peak in the warming hut. "Hi guys," he said as he sat at our table.

"What are you doing here? This mountain only has expert runs," Ron said.

"I know, I'm going to try one."

"What happened last night?" I asked.

"Interesting time, but real men don't kiss and tell."

We skied together the rest of the afternoon, but hard as we tried, Dennis remained quiet. The bus ride home differed from the ride up. The weekend had exhausted everyone. The singing, noise, and drinking on the ride to Sugarbush did not occur on the return trip.

Next Saturday, Alice and I went to the Aquarium in Baltimore and had dinner in Little Italy. I waited until she started sipping her second glass of wine, before asking, "When did Dennis leave your condo last Saturday?"

"He didn't tell you?"

"No."

"He left ten minutes after we went upstairs. Dennis told Theresa and Peggy they were nice and sexy, but that as a practicing Catholic he couldn't have sex with them."

"Really!"

"Yes. I know you and Ron would have stayed if you sat in the middle of the couch."

"No comment. What did the girls say?"

"They wondered if he was gay. They were pissed, saying they had wasted the evening on Dennis, even though he's handsome. They were looking for action as well as looks."

After we returned to work, Ron and I never asked Dennis about his evening in the townhouse condo. Two months later Dennis visited his parents in Naples, Florida. He returned beaming and walked into my office and showed me a picture of a beautiful well-tanned curvaceous Italian who looked twenty-five. "My mother introduced me to her. She's the daughter of someone she plays tennis with," Dennis said.

"Isn't she a little young?"

"No, she looks young, but she's thirty-five, four years younger than me."

"Very attractive," I said wondering why she had an interest in Dennis. He doesn't practice pre-marital sex.

"Maria had her marriage annulled just like I did. She's a practicing Catholic. I need a faithful God-fearing woman not the type I met in Sugarbush."

First, I had heard about the annulment. "Sounds serious," I said, looking at his self-satisfied grin.

"It is. We're getting married next month. She gave notice at work. The marriage bans are being announced this week in her church in Naples. We'll get married a month from Saturday."

"That was fast."

"Jerry, when you meet your true love, you know. There's no sense waiting."

Dennis returned six weeks later from his honeymoon in the British Virgin Islands and introduced his new wife to Ron and me. Maria seemed nice and a perfect fit for Dennis. We saw little of him after his marriage, especially since Ron and I spent our non-working hours with Alice and Nancy. A year after our ski trip, Ron walked into my office and proclaimed, "I'm joining Dennis."

"What do you mean?"

"I'm marrying Nancy."

"Congratulations," I said, wondering how this would affect my relationship with Alice.

"I'd like you to be my best man."

"Thanks, I look forward to the wedding. Is it going to be a big church affair?"

"No, we both had that once. We'll get married by a judge in June after she finishes teaching. We're saving money for a honeymoon trip to Rome. She'll move here and get a teaching job in Virginia."

The winter went fast. Ron, Nancy, Alice, and I went skiing at Sugarbush three times. Alice assured me many times, "Don't worry, I've been married once, I'm never getting married again. I want to be happy." The more we saw each other the less I agreed with her aversion to marriage.

Ron and Nancy's had a pleasant marriage ceremony. They held a small reception in Ron's house. Alice reminded me of her devotion to being single. Dennis attended the wedding without Maria, explaining she had to return to Florida to be with her dying father.

In August, Ron, sporting a wedding band, walked into my office grinning so much I feared he'd mash his teeth. "Guess what?"

"I'm not good at guessing. What happened?"

"Maria skipped our wedding, not because of her father, but because she and Dennis had separated."

"What? The perfect whirl-wind romance has ended?"

"Yes, do you know why they split?"

I shook my head no.

"She used to beat him," Ron said.

"Really! Why didn't he hit her back to stop it?"

"He did once, and he said she threatened to go to the police if he attacked her again."

"Poor Dennis. No courage with women."

"He had smarts and courage. When she attacked

him again, he went to the emergency room to get stitches on his left arm. When the doctor asked him what happened, he told the truth, she had stabbed him with a steak knife. The doctor had to call the police who arrested her. A judge issued a court order stating she had to leave the house and never approach Dennis again or risk going to jail. Horrified, she fled back to her parents in Florida. Dennis has filed for a divorce."

"What a story. How did you find out?"

"He told me, but made me swear to keep it to myself. Please don't tell anyone else."

"I won't. Too bad for Dennis, now with Alice and Nancy, neither of us can help him meet someone else."

Three weeks later, Dennis asked me to join him for a beer after work. He repeated what Ron told me as we sipped our beer. He ended his comments with, "I've learned my lesson. Ask your friends and never your mother to fix you up. I'll never again let the church constrict my behavior with women. I should have stayed with Theresa and Peggy that night. My life over the last year and a half would have been happier and less expensive."

"They're still available. Do you want their phone numbers?

"Yes, why do you think I'm buying you a beer?"

My Trip Alone

Almost ready to go at dawn on Friday, my car packed
with luggage and a cooler, I went back into my home
to finish one more task. I retrieved a well-used tan
canvas tote bag my deceased wife, Anne, had given
me for Christmas long ago. I loaded it with tour
guides of West Virginia, a road map of the U.S., one
novel, two non-fiction books, snacks, bottled water
and a few napkins. We always used the bag on our
car trips to Canada and the eastern and southern
United States. Every year Anne and I drove to
Canaan Valley in the third week of October to hike in
the mountains and along its fast-flowing rivers. We
loved looking at the red and golden yellow autumn
foliage. Last year I skipped the trip. She had died six
months after our last trip two years ago, and I
couldn't return so soon, still mourning her death.

This year's trip alone from St. Michaels,
Maryland to Strasburg, Virginia proceeded without

incident. As I drove, I thought about our last trip which had been an adventure. The congested traffic on the DC beltway two years ago delayed our arrival at Strasburg by an hour. At Route 48, John Marshall Highway, we exited Interstate 81 and headed west on a small two-lane highway winding through the rolling hills and rural farms in the Shenandoah Valley. The delay had made us ravenous, and we decided to stop at the first open restaurant. In a few miles, we approached Wheatfield and a large white sign with black letters proclaimed "Diner 1/4 Mile Take Right Ahead".

I remember the delight in her smile as she said, "Don't miss the turn." The restaurant had taken over part of an old garage. Its quaint charm became a pleasant memory for us. The diner served wholesome country food. Anne had a chef salad while I ate a country fried steak with fries.

When we finished lunch, the waitress asked,

"Can I get you anything else?"

"A piece of German chocolate cake please," Anne said. She had been losing weight and knew I liked her voluptuous figure so she had been eating desert daily for the last month, trying to regain it.

This trip I had the same meal, pondering if I had made the right decision to retrace our last trip, hoping to end my depression, but fearing it would drive me further into despair.

Refreshed from lunch, I drove west a few miles until Route 48 became a modern four-lane divided highway, the gateway to the West Virginia Mountains. The topography changed from rolling hills to broken, craggy and steep mountains as I entered the Appalachian plateau. Unlike two years ago when low clouds permeated the view, this day had a clear blue sky, revealing red, yellow and brown clad trees, mixed with green from the spruce and pine, adorning the peaks and valleys as far as I could see.

While the scenery on Route 48 relaxed me, dispelling any depressed thoughts, the yellow warning light on my dashboard alerted me of an impending empty gas tank. Two years ago we had panicked when we drove up to Dolly Sods and almost ran out of gas. My original plan had been to drive straight to Davis, West Virginia, at the northern end of Canaan Valley, but prudence prevailed, and I exited at Route 220, and drove south toward Moorefield. After six miles on the two-lane road I saw a gas station on my left. Returning to Route 48 with a full tank, I drove the forty miles to Davis without incident.

Anne and I drove on Route 48 after 2010 when it opened as far west as Forman east of Davis. Before 2010 we used the southern route driving through a rugged valley, containing the North Fork of the South Branch of the Potomac River. We turned west at Seneca Rocks and climbed over a rugged scenic mountain ridge. After reaching Haman, we turned north and headed into Canaan Valley. This old route while beautiful added hours to the trip. We always returned home via the equally scenic but shorter Route 50 through Maryland and Virginia.

The new highway stimulated the tourist trade, particularly skiing and hiking in Canaan Valley. However, it closed off the wonders of the original roughness of West Virginia to those who had not traveled its small winding roads.

The drive from the gas station to the old lumber town of Davis on the new highway showcased the energy basis of the West Virginia economy. Wind turbines generating electricity covered the mountain ridges northwards into Maryland. A large power plant located at the mouth of a coal mine spewed white smoke as it produced electricity. I passed strip and deep coal mines, part of the old West Virginia economy, devastated by cheap prices of their competitor—natural gas. This short drive over the high mountains concerned Anne. As an artist who painted for a living, Anne hated the removal of the mountain ridge by the strip mine shovels.

During my trip alone, the clear sky suddenly turned dark and cloudy. When I parked the car on William Avenue in Davis, snow started falling. Buildings over a hundred years old, converted to modern bars, restaurants, art galleries, and stores catering to outdoor sports, bordered the street. I walked across the street with snow flurries swirling around my head and entered the Tucker County Visitors Center. Emerging with the latest tourist information, I drove south into Canaan Valley and after ten miles arrived at my lodgings, Mountain View Resort.

Anne and I had purchased a two-story townhouse time-share there for the third week in October twenty-five years ago after our children Janet and Dennis left for college. It had two bedrooms on the second floor and sofa beds on the first that used to be filled with the sights and sounds of a happy family. Our children returned after their marriages with their pre-school-age kids. They stopped coming when school started and our mountain home returned to its annual second honeymoon site for aging empty nesters.

The memories of Anne assaulted me when I entered the house alone this year. I visualized her cooking in the kitchen, the first room I entered. When I walked into the dining room, I saw her sipping white wine, in front of the fire, whose fragrance of burning maple I remembered. The short walk up the stairs held the most memories. When I entered our bedroom, I saw her lying on the bed in a sheer white negligee, the aroma of Red Door perfume wafting from the warmth of her body, her long-blond hair sprawled over the pillow, her arms outstretched promising a renewal of our love. Unable to cope I fell on the bed and cried.

I'll never get used to the hollow sensation that starts in my stomach when I realize I'll never see, hear, smell, or touch Anne again. After five minutes of self-pity, I heard Anne's voice come to me repeating the words from her hospice bed three days before she passed, "Jack, when I die, promise me you won't. Too many spouses shut themselves in a cocoon, never wanting to meet new people or develop new experiences. Don't live in the past. You life has been too sensual to dry up. Find yourself another woman."

Trying not to cry or make her unhappy, I didn't respond.

"Promise me," she said.

Hesitating I said, "I will." But I have not. For a year I moped around the house, skipped traveling, and met no one new. Afraid to travel without Anne, I cancelled the next annual trip to West Virginia. I played tennis and golf with old friends, but had no joy when I returned to the empty house in St. Michaels. My children visited often with their kids to help cheer me up. While it did, I still dreaded sleeping alone in our bed. After listening to countless lectures by my kids, losing thirty pounds, and replaying Anne's wish to live on after her death, I planned this trip to begin my new life.

With new courage, I rose from the bed and went to the car to unpack. I took the cooler half filled compared to earlier trips, and put its contents into the refrigerator, leaving a steak on the counter for dinner. I stored the dry goods, pasta, canned tomato sauce, spices, breads, sweet potatoes and onions in the kitchen cabinets, except for one sweet potato and an onion which I left out to complement the steak. After putting my clothes away in the bedroom, I didn't experience the sadness of an hour ago, but felt glad that I had started to fulfill my promise to Anne.

The bookcases at home contained hundreds of books many of which I had read in college and graduate school forty years ago. I had started the practice of rereading old books. For this trip I brought *Slaughter House Five* by Kurt Vonnegut; *Beautiful Swimmers: Watermen, Crabs and the Chesapeake Bay* by William W. Warner, and *The Human Zoo* by Desmond Morris.

As six o'clock approached, I turned on the TV to watch the news, put the sweet potato into the microwave and began to sauté the steak and onions. The depressing news diverted my thoughts from my loneliness as I set my dinner on the coffee table and ate. Water had become my dinner beverage of choice after I realized wine did not relieve sadness but deepened it. As a left-hander, I placed a pen and pad of paper to my left and wrote plans for the rest of the trip.

As always, I planned to eat bacon and eggs to start every day. The itinerary duplicated our vacation two years ago. On Sunday, I intended to recreate the drive up Dolly Sods but this time with a full tank of gas. On Monday I'd visit Seneca Rocks. Hiking Blackwater Falls State Park would occupy Tuesday. On Wednesday I'd take a trip to Spruce Knob, the highest point in West Virginia at 4,863 feet, and then drive to explore the mountain valleys. This year while I couldn't make love I planned to sit at my laptop and begin writing this story.

On Sunday, as we did two years ago, I packed a picnic lunch planning to stop in the Dolly Sods Wildness area plateau in the Monongahela National Forest. Rather than brave the morning cold, I read *Slaughter House Five* and left at 11:00. I planned to eat a chicken salad sandwich while viewing the rugged panorama and take pictures east of Dolly Sods. Two years ago the gas tank indicator reported I had forty-four miles left before I needed gas which I had thought adequate since I only had to drive thirty miles. This year I had an almost full gas tank.

The ascent with Anne began from the southern entrance to Canaan Valley on Route 32 eastward toward FR 19 at Laneville. The route has spectacular views clear weather, like this year, or misty at the start and cloudy at the top like we experienced two years earlier.

On her last trip Anne had her camera ready, and I stopped the car when asked, as she took pictures of the small farms, white churches, shrouded valleys covered with rhododendron, and the valleys bisected with fast-flowing mountain streams as we slowly worked our way up the steep switchbacks. When we approached FR 75, the long road at the crest of Dolly Sods, the slight mist turned thicker and the visibility dropped to below a few hundred yards. Anne looked at the map and said, "I'm going to find a place to stop for lunch. Let's eat at the Red Creek Campground. It has plenty of parking. We can stop on the way and hike a few trails," Anne said.

"Rock Creek sounds good, but I don't know about hiking in this mist. We'll get soaked," I said, hoping not to dash Anne's dreams of hiking, the reason for going to Dolly Sods. I worried that my sore back had not completely recovered.

"Don't be a wimp. We have rain hats and coats in the trunk."

I nodded okay, willing to take a minor discomfort to keep her smiling.

As we drove, Anne noticed all the small trail-head parking lots filled with pickup trucks and the side of road covered with men in wet-weather hunting clothes. The density of the hunters on both sides of the road increased as we drove north. Curious, I stopped and questioned two hunters.

"What are you hunting?"

"Blue grouse."

"Are this many hunters always here?"

"They'd be more this time of year if it was warmer."

As we left, I glanced at the remaining fuel indicator gauge, shocked that it showed only twenty-one miles remaining. Anne noticed my concern and said, "What's the matter?"

"We've only driven ten miles. The gauge reports we've used up over half our gas."

As we approached Rock Creek, Anne said, "My back's hurting. Maybe hiking isn't a good idea."

"You'll feel better after lunch," I said, trying not to smile at avoiding walking the mist covered trails.

Ten minutes later, we arrived at the picnic area and found the parking lot full.

The fuel gauge hadn't gone down as much as before, now registering sixteen miles.

"Let's find a gas station and then worry about eating," Anne said looking at the dashboard.

"Okay,"

"Do you want to eat while you're driving?" Anne asked.

"No, I'm not famished, and I want to keep my

eye on the road. I don't want to hit any of the parked cars or kill a hunter."

"Good, there's more of them than us. They'd retaliate with their guns and since we're almost out of gas we'd never get away."

Anne always had a great sense of humor.

"I'll be careful and drive slowly to conserve gas. I'll exit at the first right turn directing us out of the park and drive to the valley until we find a gas station."

"Don't take too long, I'm not so good. I'm full of gas and need a restroom. If there weren't so many hunters I'd go behind a tree."

Both of us would have twenty years earlier. The strained look on Anne's face worried me. Anne never complained, and only mentioned being sick when she had a serious illness.

After driving five more minutes, I said, "The exit must be close." The gas indicator gauge had gone down to thirteen miles. Anne noticed my concern but said nothing

When you love someone sick, you experience their pain if you cannot help them. I panicked looking for the exit to the valley. After another ten minutes of driving I noticed a sign, stating the wildness area would end and to turn right at State Road 4. As I started the descent the mileage available indicator fell to nine miles when the mist cleared. Anne noticing my concern remained quiet. We drove for another six miles when a gas station appeared out of the wilderness. Anne yelled, "Thank God," and rushed into the combination gas, grocery and hunting/fishing store while I filled the tank. She returned smiling.

"I'm hungry." She said. Her answer told me she had recovered. We parked next to the store, and I walked to a picnic table carrying the cooler. Anne went into the store and returned with two cold beers. "We're out of the mountains. Let's celebrate."

The destination of day two, Seneca Rocks, always amazed me. Thirty years ago, Anne and I used to climb its rock cliffs with ropes. We passed that stage long ago and substituted the technical climb with a hike up the path and wood stairway on the left side of the rocks.

I still remember our first trip over thirty years ago. Ned, our climbing instructor, asked as we finished climbing, "Do these mountains remind you of anything?"

We both remained silent.

"I'll give you another hint. What's the name of the general store across the street?"

We both looked and said, "Yokum?"

"Nothing! Just look around the tops of the mountain ridges and think of your childhood," Ned said.

I hadn't a clue. Anne jumped up and down laughing and said, "Li'l Abner."

"That's it," Ned said.

Of course! I thought as I scanned the mountains, remembering the joy of reading his adventures in the colored comics of the Sunday newspapers.

Anne and I always ate a picnic lunch after climbing. We sat on a blanket watching the North Fork of the South Branch of the Potomac River flow past the rocks. We carried on this tradition even after we switched from technical climbing to hiking up the prepared mountain trail.

Two months ago before the trip with Anne, I had just recovered from a pinched sciatic nerve that made it painful to walk long distances. As I hiked toward the trail, Anne said, "Are you sure you're up to this?"

"Yes," I said, not knowing if my legs agreed with my reply.

"Okay, go ahead. I'll follow you."

While I walked uphill at a slow pace, I started sweating as I struggled to breathe the county air which at five hundred feet, could not be short of oxygen. After a few hundred yards, I sat on a rock hoping to bring my heart rate back to normal.

Anne sat next to me, "Do you want to go back?"

The male ego can sometimes be a terrible and foolish thing, "No. I'll just go slow and pace myself."

"Jack, you're out of shape. You haven't exercised since you hurt your back. You just can't start in again. It's dangerous."

"No. I'm okay," I said despite realizing she spoke the truth. Even though I had gained ten pounds, no one could tell me I couldn't walk up a path I used to scamper up like a five-year-old twenty years ago.

After I caught my breath, we started again, following the trail which included fallen logs and switchbacks. The more we walked the steeper the trail became. I stopped to rest at the one-quarter marker. Anne sat next to me, handing me a water bottle, and said, "Here drink this, you don't want to get dehydrated. I don't feel that good. If you want to turn back, I won't mind."

"Let me rest. I want to continue," I said as I chugged the bottle. After a few minutes my heart rate had subsided and my pulse returned to normal. I started walking again. Anne followed and told me she worried about how she would get me down to the bottom if I collapsed. After a hundred yards my heart raced. I sat on a log. "Anne, I'm sorry, I can't make it. You go ahead."

"What, and have a coyote or a bear eat you for lunch, or worse have Daisy Mae's granddaughter whisk you off to her cabin and subject you to unbearable sexual pleasures for the next few weeks? No sir, I'm staying with you."

My pain subsided when I realized in my physical state I'd pass out after one minute of sexual torture and that my wife loved me and would protect me. We strolled down the trail. At the end she said, "Find a place to put down the blanket," and went to the car to retrieve the cooler. I wondered if at my age, I could induce a heart attack by stupidity. I knew it would be hard for me to live if Anne passed before me, but I never thought of my going first. She and I with over forty years together had melded.

When she returned she handed me a beer and said, "Drink this. You'll need the potassium for your heart."

I didn't argue, but sat on the blanket and accepted a chicken salad sandwich. Looking at her I said, "After all this time, I still love you."

"I know, but I do too."

Both of us smiled at each other while finishing lunch.

This year, after playing tennis two or three times a week, going to the gym faithfully and eating healthy food I had lost the weight I had gained. I looked forward to the hike and made it to the top only having had to stop once in the cool October air. On the ascent and descent, memories of Anne and me laughing, walking, and holding hands filled my mind as I passed way points on the trail.

On Tuesday morning after having a great dinner

the night before at The Golden Anchor and finishing *Slaughter House Five* I started my day at Blackwater Falls State Park. I retrieved an old map of the park to plan my hiking route, the same Anne and I tried to finish two years ago.

Our day had begun by parking at the closed Harold S. Walters Nature Center at ten. We wore ski jackets to protect us from the chill of the cold crisp air and from the light mist that pervaded the park that morning. We hiked the Dobbin House Trail, along the ridge of the Blackwater Canyon till it turned into the Pase Point Trail, and ended at an outlook over Blackwater Canyon. Anne set a slow pace, stopping to gaze at the different views and inhaling the fall odors. Since we walk slowly, I didn't get tired as I earlier had on the hike up Seneca Rocks. Many couples, holding hands like ourselves, and families with inquisitive children, accompanied us on our walk. The view from the outlook into the three hundred foot deep canyon, while always spectacular, differed every time we visited it, depending on the season, the strength of the sunlight, the moisture in the air, and the color of the leaves or lack of them. I must have over a hundred pictures of this scenery.

Anne loved nature and took pictures of the squirrels, birds, and deer we spied on our morning walk. While on occasion we heard the growl of a bear, we never saw one. Most hikers in the

Appalachian Mountains believe that bears fear humans more than we fear them, leading them to flee when they hear us. It sounds good. I wondered what would happen if Anne and I came upon a deaf bear.

On our return we went south on the Pendleton Trace Trail before reaching the parking lot for a short walk to the Pendleton Point Overlook. This vista always dazzled us with the eyes of a couple who had spent the last twenty years on the flatland farms, marshes, and small towns of the Delmarva Peninsula.

Our stomachs always told us at the overlook we needed to eat. We stopped in a picnic area close to and east of the overlook. The sodas and roast beef sandwiches replenished us for our short walk to the crowning glory of the park, Blackwater Falls.

The morning events of this year's trip to the picnic area paralleled those two years earlier, except I missed Anne's sweet voice. I reminisced of our last trip recalling her comments and jokes. I arrived at the picnic area an hour earlier than the previous trip, not being accompanied by a strolling lover.

Two years ago Anne and I walked back to the car and drove to the parking lot near the Trading Post to prepare for our walk down the wooden steps to view Blackwater Falls. As I parked the car, I saw Anne grimace as she unhooked her seat belt.

"Are you okay?" I asked.

"Just a small dull stomach pain."

"We can skip the walk to the falls. We've seen it dozens of times."

"No, it's not that bad. It's what I look forward to each year."

"If your pain increases we can stop anytime."

She didn't answer, but led the way. Lovingly, I followed, smiling and listening to the roar of the water falling over sixty feet and crashing into the pool at the bottom. She turned and looked at me, her face glowing with anticipation of standing across from the falls. We held hands, with the camera in my pocket to protect it from mist as the water crashed over the rocks. She held the banister of the wooden stairs to protect herself from slipping on the mist-saturated steps.

Three quarters of the way down, where the stairway turned and stood over the river, Anne shook and snatched her hand from the banister and gripped her stomach. Her feet slipped, she fell hitting her head on walkway. Her forward motion propelled her body toward the open space over the river. My grip instinctively held her arm as her legs and hips dangled in the open air. A well-built young man walking behind me acted without hesitation, dropped to the surface of the walkway and grabbed under her other arm and pulled her to safety. The fall had knocked Anne out and she took several minutes to wake up. A crowd surrounded us trying to see what happened.

The man who had help save her told the crowd to move back, took out his cell phone and called 911.

The park police appeared in minutes. One asked,

"What happened?"

I explained her fall and pointed to the gentleman who had helped. He said, "I'm Ted Kowalski, I am an Emergency Medical Responder and watched her head bounce off the wood. She might have a concussion."

The police summoned an ambulance which arrived as Anne reached the parking lot, carried up the stairs by the police. I thanked Kowalski for his help and followed the ambulance to Davis Memorial Hospital at Elkins forty miles away.

I waited in the Emergency Room lobby while they wheeled her into the examination rooms. After forty-five minutes a Dr. Hanson introduced himself and said. "She doesn't have a concussion. We treated abrasions on the back of her head and legs. However, we're concerned about her stomach pain, nausea and diarrhea. She's undergoing an MRI to find out if it's serious. We should know in an hour."

He returned to the Emergency Room. I sat stunned. I loved Anne, but one of her faults annoyed me. She never admitted pain and unless deathly sick would not change our plans.

An hour later an attendant approached and asked

me to follow him to visit my wife. When I entered her room, Dr. Hansen turned from pointing at an MRI picture of Anne's insides and said, "Just showing your wife two spots we found on her pancreas." He pointed them out. "We don't know what they are, but they should be examined as soon as possible. I've called Anne's physician and made an appointment for tomorrow afternoon at 4:00 p.m. at the Anne Arundel Medical Center in Annapolis. We're not going to keep her here. Good luck on the diagnosis."

Anne didn't smile as we left the hospital. During our drive back to our townhouse, she said. "I'm sorry I ruined our vacation."

"You didn't ruin it. Your health is more important than hiking in West Virginia for the thirtieth time. Let's leave this afternoon so we don't have an exhausting drive tomorrow."

"Okay. But I'll be thinking of the diagnosis tonight and tomorrow. I hope it's not cancer." She had expressed my greatest fear. "It's almost a hundred percent fatal," she continued.

"That's only one possibility," I said.

She smiled, "I know dear. One nice thing about us, we always try to make each other happy."

We didn't talk for the rest of the drive back to the townhouse. When we left Canaan Valley I planned to drive as far as I could before getting hungry or tired. At Manassas, Virginia I pulled off Interstate 66 and checked into a Days Inn.

Anne had her laptop opened and running when I woke up at 7:00. She heard me move, looked over and said, "I'm searching for my diagnostic possibilities. I don't want to be blindsided after 4:00 p.m., when they stitch me up after the biopsy and tell me what they've found."

Anne always impressed me with her positive outlook.

The news at the hospital devastated us. Anne had stage 4 pancreatic cancer. Up to then my life really never had a crisis. Both our careers allowed us to save for a financially secure retirement. Our children married well, flourished in their careers and gave us beautiful grandchildren. I never had to grieve over my dying parents, as my peers did, since they died in my twenties. Unprepared for her death, I struggled for the next six months of her life. She understood my unhappiness, and her final words at the hospice advised me not to join her, but start a new life. After a year of brooding I recovered, helped by my children. I planned the trip alone to cement my memory of Anne, end my depression, and transition into a new life to fulfill my commitment.

When I sat alone at the picnic table, I ate lunch and reread *Beautiful Swimmers*. Turning to page thirty-eight I heard, "Jack! What are you doing here?"

I looked up at an attractive woman with red hair close to my age standing over me. "Hi Ronnie, I come here every year. I have a time share. I haven't seen you in a long time."

"Three years. I'm sorry about Anne. How are you doing?"

"I miss her. At first it devastated me. She told me to move on. I'm here repeating a trip we did annually, trying to start a new life."

"Are you alone?"

"Yes, I haven't developed the courage to start dating. How about you?"

"My recovery is further along than yours. Ben died three years ago. I'm here with three other widows. We're going to hike to the falls. Would you like to join us?"

****

Thank you for reading *First Time*. If you liked the book, or my other books, please write an Amazon review to inform other potential readers they would enjoy the book. Please open my Amazon author page to access the forms to write your review.

https://www.amazon.com/Frank-E.-Hopkins/e/B0028AR904

Chick on the book cover of the book you want to review and the review option will the page bottom.

About the Author

Frank E Hopkins writes realistic crime novels and short stories portraying social and political issues.

Frank was raised in the New York City area, went to Graduate School at the University of Maryland, earned a Ph.D. in Economics, taught for ten years at Binghamton University in upstate New York, and returned to the DC suburbs. He moved to the Delaware beaches in 2001. He used settings from all his locations in his writing. He has published five novels: *The Counterfeit Drug Murders* which won third place in the novel category in Delaware Press Associations 2021 Communications Contest, *The Billion Dollar Embezzlement Murders* which won third place in the novel category in Delaware Press Associations 2020 Communications Contest, *Abandoned Homes: Vietnam Revenge Murders* which won first place in the mystery/thriller category in the Maryland Writers Association 2018 novel contest, *The Opportunity*, and *Unplanned Choices*. Frank's collection of short stories, *First Time*, was awarded second place for a single author collection in the Delaware Press Associations 2017 Communication Contest.

Frank is active in the Rehoboth Bay Writers Guild, the Eastern Shore Writers Association, the Delaware Writers Network, and Mystery Writers of America, and the Berlin chapter of the Maryland Writers Association.

Website: www.frankehopkins.com

ABOUT THE AUTHOR

Author email address: frank@frankehopkins.com

Facebook profile: http://facebook.com/hopkinsfe

Hoffman and O'Hare Mystery Series

The Counterfeit Drug Murders, the third novel in the Hoffman and O'Hare Mystery Series, is a sequel to *The Billion Dollar Embezzlement Murders* and *Abandoned Homes: Vietnam Revenge Murders*. All three books have been structured so they can be read independently.

The Maryland Writers Association awarded *Abandoned Homes: Vietnam Revenge Murders* first place in the mystery/thriller in their 2018 novel contest. *The Billion Dollar Embezzlement Murders* won third place in the novel category in the Delaware Press Association's 2020 Communications Contest. This sequel does not continue a discussion of the crimes in *Abandoned Homes: Vietnam Revenge Murders*, but follows the lives of the two main characters of the book: Margaret Hoffman retired detective Delaware State Police, and Paul O'Hare, retired professor.

In the first novel, the couple meets and falls in love as Detective Hoffman leads the Delaware State Police team to solve the murders. Hoffman and O'Hare write a best-selling book about the revenge murders.

In the second novel, they marry and after Detective Hoffman retires from the State Police, they participate in solving the embezzlement, and become targets of the murderers in Greece on their honeymoon and on the Outer Banks of North Carolina.

In *The Counterfeit Drug Murders,* a close friend of the

two detectives dies from tainted counterfeit prescription drugs. Further research indicates their friends' deaths are part of a larger tragedy, including the demise of several individuals from the same drug. The detectives vow to solve the cause of the death of their friend.

FRANK E HOPKINS

The Counterfeit Drug Murders

The Counterfeit Drug Murders is the third novel in the Hoffman and O'Hare Mystery Series. The premature heart failure of the matriarch, Mary, tore the Jewel family apart. Mary's children and her cardiologist did not accept that Mary had died a natural death in Duck, North Carolina. Brian, Mary's son, clinically depressed by his mother's death, recruited detectives Hoffman and O'Hare to discover who murdered Mary. A decade earlier, an immoral physician had enslaved her daughter, Eve, into opioid addiction – Mary's death awoke a long simmering hatred.

Eve independently imposed her retribution on the pharmaceutical industry risking life in prison. Eve's revenge involved cyber techniques to identify, locate, and track her victims. Eve mentally struggles with being caught and losing her lover or continuing her self-justified revenge.

The detectives discover Mary's killer might have participated in other murders related to counterfeit drugs. They pursue the serial killer as he and his lover flee the police. The interstate search for the murderer leads to a fatal car chase through steep and dangerous mountain roads. Who will survive?

Readers of this pharmaceutical thriller/mystery have stated: it is riveting, twisty realism, loved the detail, could not put the book down, emotional read, very timely story, a delightful read, a new type of murder in the midst of the opioid crisis, and easy to read.

What readers think of *The Counterfeit Drug Murders*

Great mystery that leads you into a new venue of illicit drug companies.

Frank has written yet another terrific mystery. He continues to develop the main characters of the series and also to draw us in with new and interesting people. The story took me to many familiar places which is always entertaining. Frank leaves the reader wanting more knowing the latest character has a lot yet to do. Which way will Eve go? Only Frank knows for sure. By Diana McDonough on February 8, 2021

A Police Procedural with a Very Real Issue

The Counterfeit Drug Murders is another Hoffman and O'Hare Mystery that provides both an excellent police procedural, as do the previous installments, and an exploration into the world of counterfeit drugs, a serious and very much real issue. Although the story involves Hoffman and O'Hare, The Counterfeit Drug Murders introduces new characters into the mix around which much of the story revolves. As before in the series, the story takes the readers to a variety of locations. Both intriguing and educational, I recommend the book. By Jackson Coppley on January 10, 2021

A New Type of Murder

Frank Hopkins writes like Sergeant Joe Friday, "Just the facts, M'am" as the writer's fictional detective husband and wife team of Hoffman and O'Hare tackle a series of murders related to poison drugs. Carefully documented charts and tallies of deaths entice the reader to follow clues leading to other clues. At the same time, the author's expertise puts us into the head of an unknown person tracing down the killers, and we begin to cheer for success. The book is hard to put down as the killers try to escape justice in exciting attempts and the person, still not known by the law, hunts them down. Hopkins knows his subject and brings to light a growing problem of careless and criminal drug compounding killing many patients. No longer can a reader trust for sure the drugs in the little plastic bottles given out usually innocently at the pharmacy. By Thomas Hollyday on January 30, 2021

Emotional read

Very intense and very emotionally gripping experience. It develops in the way that surprised the hell out of me.

But it was good. Well told for sure. By Nan on January 15, 2021

A delightful read

An interesting read the story revolves around a series of murders related to drug poisoning, and detective Hoffman and her husband O'Hare try to solve this mystery. The plot is well written, and the author very carefully plotted the cues and clues of the murders for the reader to hook them with the book. And the way the author explains every detail, like the procedure to find the clues and the methods they follow it actually ignites your imagination. This is one of the books in a series called "Hoffman and O'Hare mystery," but you can read it as a single book as well. The author also brings up a sensitive issue of counterfeit drugs and the underground world of pharmaceuticals that I was not at all aware of. So it is kind of educational for me as well. Overall it is a great book to read. I would definitely recommend this book to anyone. By JC on February 8, 2021

Twisted Realism

Heavy doses of realism and well-plotted twists make this police procedural a page-turner. By LindsVan on January 20, 2021

FRANK E HOPKINS

The Billion Dollar Embezzlement Murders

The thriller sequel to *Abandoned Homes: Vietnam Revenge Murders* starts with the heinous murder of a participant in a billion dollar embezzlement of a Delaware company, the Liberty Credit Card Co. The action switches to the continuing romance of Margaret Hoffman and Paul O'Hare started in the first novel. They marry, have a successful release of the book they wrote about the abandoned home murders, and decide to spend their honeymoon in Greece.

The embezzlement continues as the crime's ringleader, Hank Strong, orders the murder of Jean Cummings, who discovered the crime. She avoids the first two attacks, at her home and at a mountain cabin in West Virginia, but fearing for her life she flies to Greece to enlist the help of Margaret and Paul to help solve the crime. As they become involved, an attempt is also made on the authors' lives in Mykonos, Greece and Duck, North Carolina. The action returns to the U.S. as the Delaware and Greek police get closer to solving the crime. The embezzlers make plans to leave the U.S. to live in a country without an extradition treaty with the U.S. Will the police or the embezzlers be successful in their quests?

What readers think of *The Billion Dollar Embezzlement Murders*

It Will Keep You Up All Night.

Move over Elvirah and Willie. Frank Hopkins has created a pair of sleuths to rival the Higgins-Clark duo, adding the distinction of their being published authors. If you follow Margaret and Paul through this embezzlement scam, you will not only be rewarded with a gripping thriller, but you'll also take away an education in Finance and Geography. Hopkins's Ph.D. in Economics gives him the authority to fine-tune the shenanigans of his characters so as to distill them down to the understanding of everyman... You don't want to miss this one. Mary D. on June 22, 2019

Cybercrime is real!

This is a fictional tale of a very REAL, real world issue. Cybercrime and digital currency theft and manipulation. I always get a kick out of reading stories of these types of character. And our main "villain" in this case is enjoyable to read. Great writing, fast paced, and it's definitely a page-turner. I hate spoilers so I won't give any. Jnmorrison on September 4, 2020.

Wow! A look into cyber-crime!

Okay, this introduces the reader to a very realistic type of crime that could happen in the world we live in--or it lays out how it could. It is almost like a real-time peek into something very real. Written in a style that enhances the plot and the characters--giving the reader a somewhat detached view, it really comes together and keeps you entertained and turning the page. This is the type of book you want to read when you feel like a mystery or some drama. Grab a cup of coffee and open this one up. If you like mysteries, you're going to enjoy this ride. Addon on September 27, 2020

Take a Ride with Hoffman and O'Hare

They met in *Abandoned Homes*, and now they're back for more action. *The Billion Dollar Embezzlement Murders* takes us for a ride with Hoffman and O'Hare, the best pair of sleuths since Nick and Nora. The stakes are high. Bad guys get testy when there's a billion dollars at stake. Hopkins does a good job in describing action and in setting scenes and this book has plenty of action. Take a read and get involved with Hoffman and O'Hare. Jackson Coppley on June 8, 2019

A Compelling International Thriller

Set partly in the U.S. and partly in Greece, THE BILLION DOLLAR EMBEZZLEMENT MURDERS is the second book of a thriller series featuring Delaware State Police Detective Margaret Hoffman (now retired), and retired professor Paul O'Hare.

Recently married, they're thoroughly enjoying their

newlywed status and the bestseller success of the true crime book they wrote about the case they solved in Book #1 of the series. Now in Book #2 they've got a new case to solve and write about, the embezzlement of $1 billion from one of the top financial services firms in the country and the brutal murders committed to cover up the crime.

A complex, well-plotted, well-researched thriller that's vastly entertaining and enjoyable. The main characters are charming and likeable, and it's fun to follow them on their death-defying adventures – especially when they take us on a fabulous insider's tour of the Grecian Islands. Fascinating, authentic-sounding details about financial data, systems, and security, and the ingenious embezzlement plan.

Keeps you turning the pages – or tapping your Kindle – all the way to the satisfying conclusion. Definitely recommended. Kristy Dark on April 19, 2020

Well Thought-out Crime Thriller

I really liked this book because of the embezzlement scheme being so interesting. The author provided just enough details to keep me guessing. The Greek setting was a nice touch. I will definitely go back and read the first book in the series now that I know the characters who are very likable. Reader88 on May 12, 2020

It was a fun read on different levels

Not only was I invested in the story's characters, but I have been a lot of the places that were settings and found myself reliving past adventures. Well done! Fast paced. Great use of language. All in all, I am going to buy the first in this series which I had missed and keep with it. Excellent book! EH Ivans on August 31, 2020

Great Read

Margaret and Paul are back: married, happy and enjoying the good life in Greece. But, their bliss gets blitzed when a massive embezzlement scheme in their native Delaware is uncovered and follows them to Greece. As they assist their friend, they find themselves targets for elimination also. Frank Hopkins continues the fast-paced action for this pair we first met in *Abandoned Homes: The Vietnam Revenge Murders*. William Kennedy on July 22, 2019.

Another great novel from Frank Hopkins!

I was most impressed with the amount of research that Frank Hopkins must have done to write *The Billion Dollar Embezzlement Murders*. The technical aspects of embezzling that amount of money were well described. His depiction of Greece and its many islands made you feel you were there. Being a Delawarean, I was familiar with many of the other locales throughout the book, which added to the verisimilitude. And, of course, the plot was spot-on and moved quickly. Highly recommended! F. Weldon Burge on July 4, 2019

A good read

The Billion Dollar Embezzlement Murders held my attention from the first page to the very end. I liked the flipping between the different characters trying to solve the crimes to the perpetrators still committing them. The description of the scenery only adds to the enjoyment as the story journeys across the world. Amy on June 14, 2019

Unique mystery!

Just finished reading Frank Hopkins latest novel *The Billion Dollar Embezzlement Murders*. This mystery is filled with high-tech crime -- murder -- back stabbing intrigues and Greece. No putting this story down as it is a straight read through. Bill on September 20 2019

They're Back!

An unlikely pair at first, Frank Hopkins new dynamic duo, Hoffman and O'Hare are fast becoming super sleuths. Professor and cop, now writers, travel to Greece and uncover the crooks behind *The Billion Dollar Embezzlement Murders*. Crooks who also happen to be murderers. Frank Hopkins second novel featuring Hoffman and O'Hare has them in a fast-paced race to discover the murderers before they become the next victims. Amazon Customer on May 28, 2019.

Abandoned Homes: Vietnam Revenge Murders

IS A SUSPENSEFUL SERIAL KILLER CRIME NOVEL

U.S. involvement in the Vietnam War ended in 1975 when the U.S. abandoned its Embassy in Saigon. However, the hate developed during the war years, especially at major universities continued. Proponents of the war, fierce opponents of communism, acted during the war years to remove potential traitors from our society. Those against the war continued their opposition, begun in the 1960s, culminating in the riots and student killings at major universities, including Kent State, the University of Maryland and the University of Wisconsin-Madison.

Paul O'Hare, a retired history professor, uncovers a long-hidden domestic impact of the Vietnam War thirty-five years after the war ended when he finds a skeleton in the crawl space of an abandoned home in southern Delaware. The Delaware State Police investigation team, headed by Detective Margaret Hoffman, discovers two more skeletons, and the quest for a serial killer begins. Hoffman soon discovers the three skeletons had been graduate students at the University of Maryland during the 1970s as had Paul O'Hare, who becomes a major suspect. Eventually the State Police clear him, and he begins a romantic relationship with Detective Hoffman that includes conflicts between his anti-war sentiments and her experience as a Marine veteran.

The search for a serial killer reveals a complex web of interrelated former students, a crusading newspaper reporter, and CIA agents and double agents, in this fast-paced suspense novel.

The Maryland Writers Association awarded *Abandoned Homes: Vietnam Revenge Murders* first place in the mystery/thriller category in their 2018 Communications Contest.

What readers say about *Abandoned Homes: Vietnam Revenge Murders*

A Mystery on Many Levels

Frank Hopkins spins a tale that begins one place and takes you to another as the story unfolds. A photographer finds interest in old houses in the countryside where properties are low value and the houses are forgotten and left to decay. He steps on rotten boards exposing a skeleton and discovering the source of a deadly virus. So, we have an outbreak menace story, right? Wrong. As a smart, tough policewoman becomes involved, we have a cold case story about who the skeleton represented and now have a murder mystery. The murderers are alive and remain dangerous. The photographer and the policewoman begin a relationship and you want to know where that goes. Jack Coppley on November 4, 2017.

I fell in love with the two main characters
Once I started this book I could not put it down. I fell in love with the two main characters. The story moved fast so you don't have time to get bored. The characters, the locations and the events were all believable. This is the third book of Mr. Hopkins that I have read and am now starting on the fourth. This gentleman is definitely my new favorite author. Bonnie P Cashell on January 4, 2018.

Good Story, Especially for Delawareans!
This was a fast moving mystery and easy to read, with no dull chapters. I found the subject matter enlightening as well. Carol70 on February 5, 2018

Frank Hopkins Scores Another Hit
Whoever said that reading was either for education or enjoyment hasn't read Frank Hopkins' novels. This second entry into a developing series has all the elements of a gripping detective yarn designed to keep you glued to its pages. At the same time you'll learn, as an old forties song goes, "A little bit about a lot of things." This latter point may be a coincidence, but

the Hopkins style brings to mind crusty gum shoes of mid-century American noir, Sam Spade, Mickey Spillane and Perry Mason. Although his protagonist, Margaret Hoffman, may be more closely aligned with later women characters like Kinsey Milhone and Jessica Fletcher.

This novel spans the years from the end of the Vietnam War in 1975 to the present, and gradually reveals a murderous plot involving pro and anti-war factions resulting in a series of heinous crimes. Rat-infested basements and crawl spaces of abandoned houses reveal the grisly remains of the victims and soon connections are discovered among the skeletons.

Although himself a suspect at first in these crimes, Paul O'Hare helps Detective Hoffman unravel the mystery and the couple begin their partnership, professional and personal. If you haven't read either Hoffman - O'Hare Novel, read this one first for continuity.

Not only did I enjoy the edge-of-my-seat aspects of the book, I learned a lot about my own neighboring states. Frank clearly travels to his novels' locations doing exhaustive research. You'll travel south through sleepy towns in Delaware and stopping for lunch in an historic Virginia waterfront village. And as with all Hopkins' novels, you'll always know what his characters ordered from the menu. My suggested selection for you is *Abandoned Homes: Vietnam Revenge Murders*. Order it now while you're on the Amazon site. It couldn't be easier. What won't be as easy is putting it down. Mary D on August 28, 2019

Skeletons in the basement and closet

Frank Hopkins has managed to reach back in time to rekindle old hates and awaken fears in his latest novel, *Abandoned Homes: Vietnam Revenge Murders*. Beauty, skill and toughness in the person of State Police Detective Margaret Hoffman, retired U.S. Marine, combine with modern police forensics to solve decades-old murders involving the CIA. Threading her way through the trail of skeletons, she falls in love with Paul O'Hare, a retired history professor, who initially discovered the skeletons, only to become a murder suspect. Follow the trail of mystery, motive and murder that abounded on college campuses of the 1970s. Amazon Customer on October 13, 2017.

Unpredictable...Informative...Entertaining

Abandoned Homes: Vietnam Revenge Murders is a complex murder mystery which holds you captive from the onset. Hopkins' hero begins an unforgettable journey into the unknown with the discovery of a skeleton in an abandoned home. The story unfolds as he works in tandem with the Delaware State Police to ascertain the identity of the victim. It soon becomes clear that the political unrest of the Vietnam War is a pivotal piece of the puzzle. College campuses were a focal point of the peace movement and it was determined that the victim was a student at the University of Maryland during the 1970s. As a witness to the protest of the Vietnam War while attending the University of Maryland in 1970, Hopkins lends a personal aspect to his narrative, which is relevant in all of his books. Brimming with twists and turns! A Must Read! Linda D. on October 6, 2017.

Another good read from Hopkins

Hopkins shows us his versatility with a murder mystery this time. The story develops when a retired college professor stumbles across a dead body in an abandoned home he's researching. First, he's a suspect by the investigating female State Police officer, he then becomes her lover. They follow leads across the Mid-Atlantic States to uncover a long-buried plot that began in the political unrest of the Vietnam War. Each chapter takes the reader deeper into this complex tale of intrigue. William Kennedy on October 21, 2017.

Hatred between factions for and against the Viet Nam war didn't end when the war did

In Frank Hopkins' new murder mystery *Abandoned Homes: Vietnam Revenge Murders*, a retired history professor pursues an unusual but innocent hobby-investigating and photographing abandoned homes in rural Delaware. His discovery of skeletons in the abandoned homes sets off a search for a serial killer that endangers his life as it reawakens the raging conflicts that took place on college campuses during the Viet Nam war years. Carole Ottesen on November 17, 2017.

Hard to put down!

Such a devious mystery! Frank E. Hopkins has a way of weaving an intriguing story along with characters that stick in your head. Kari on January 5, 2018.

I enjoyed this captivating tale

Mysteries are not normally my genre, but the author kept my attention throughout. Can't wait to read his next book! Diana M. on January 5, 2018.

Another great book by Frank Hopkins

Frank Hopkins' intriguing book *Abandoned Homes: Vietnam Revenge Murders* is a step-by step murder mystery. From the first page to the last, it is a fast paced story that is difficult to put down. The book starts innocently when Paul O'Hare, a retired history professor, stumbles upon skeletons in an abandoned house which he is photographing. Paul meets Detective Margaret Hoffman who is on the case using modern day forensics. Even though he becomes a suspect, Margaret Hoffman and Paul become lovers. Not only is this book a riveting tale of murder, but also has a great romance. Something for everyone! If you want an entertaining and unpredictable book, then this is definitely for you. S. Scarangella on March 11, 2018.

Mesmerizing Murder Mystery

Mesmerizing is the word for this book. The mystery story line was exceptionally creative and from the beginning draws the reader in one direction, and veers off smoothly into others before its surprise ending. One could not help but sympathize with the corpses and surprisingly the culprits. The book brought back memories of our confused country over the Vietnam anti-war movement and my own College Park experience. My only complaint is that the "lovely" heroine policewoman's food choices were entirely too healthy!!!! Kathy H on March 15, 2018.

Great mystery murder investigation

Excellent mystery with a strong female lead character. The Delmarva location setting and description are an interesting backdrop for this novel. A book you will not want to put down until the mystery is solved. Kathy L. on March 25, 2018.

Abandoned Homes: Vietnam Revenge Murders is a page-turner!

In the late 1960s and early 1970s college campuses across the United States were sites of anti-war protests sometimes accompanied by violence as students and the country divided over the war in Vietnam. In 2008, when retired University of Maryland history professor, Paul O'Hare stumbles upon two skeletons in an abandoned home he's photographing in lower Delaware, he suddenly and inexplicably finds himself at the center of an intense and long-ranging police investigation. Paul is eventually cleared, but as the police uncover more and more evidence leading to the identity of the real killer, old enmities and enemies emerge from the shadows of Paul's past, making him a target right up to the story's dramatic conclusion. *Abandoned Homes: Vietnam Revenge Murders* is a step-by-step police procedural page-turner. Recommended for fans of realistic detective fiction, with a bonus if the reader is from Delaware and can recognize locations and landmarks! JM Reinbold on June 22, 2018.

Nicely crafted murder mystery

A masterfully written police procedural, with finely defined characters and a well-paced plot. Hopkins has clearly done his research. And, as a Delawarean, I enjoyed his many references to lower Delaware and the beach area--many locales of which I recognize and have visited. The scenes of violence are handled with precision and with modicum gore. Two thumbs up. F. Weldon Burge on October 10, 2018

Many of the locations in this book are easily recognizable to readers in the Mid-Atlantic area

Frank Hopkins' book, *Abandoned Homes: Vietnam Revenge Murders*, looks back at the turmoil, deception, intrigue, and anger of the late sixties and early seventies in this engrossing, hard to put down mystery. It won first place for a mystery/thriller novel in the 2018 Maryland Writers' Association novel contest. It is a thought-provoking, exciting mostly police procedural with a little romance thrown in. Many of the locations in this book are easily recognizable to readers in the Mid-Atlantic area. Eileen Haavik McIntire on July 5, 2018

Stirs your curiosity

If you are looking for a mystery that stirs your curiosity throughout, *Abandoned Homes: Vietnam Revenge Murders* is definitely one to purchase. From the beginning, Mr. Hopkins sets the stage with vivid images of rural Delaware through which he skillfully creates an intricate web of characters and plot twists that connect skeletons found in deserted houses to polarized views of the Vietnam War. You, too, will enjoy reading how the pieces of the puzzle fit together. A great read! JD, an avid reader on April 15, 2018

Engaging

Very engaging story and believable characters. This is also a Maryland Writer's Association winner, and Frank did a great job. F. J. Talley on June 17, 2018

...a fast paced story of mystery and murder

Abandoned Homes: Vietnam Revenge Murders is a fast paced story of mystery and murder. The author wastes no time with preliminaries and takes us directly to our hero who discovers several murders that have not been solved. He reports finding the bodies, one by one, but ironically, he finds himself a suspect. The story is set primarily during the heart of the Vietnam War during the 1960s and focuses on the conflict people feel about being involved in this war. This story held my attention throughout. Whether you're into murder mystery or not, I think you will enjoy reading this book. I highly recommend it. ruthziemniak on January 29, 2020

Made in the USA
Columbia, SC
09 July 2024

38217672R00140